TWO MINUTES FOR HOLDING

S.L. STERLING

TWO MINUTES FOR HOLDING

by

S.L. Sterling

©2025

Chapter One

Peyton - Two Months Earlier

My fucking brother! Sorry half-brother! Anger boiled inside of me. Who the fuck did he think he was? Holding me while mall security was going to be breathing down my neck in a matter of seconds. I knew I should have just taken off. It had just shocked me so much when the security system had gone off. Figures the first time I take something I get caught. Then Knox, in all his mighty glory, had to look over in my direction.

Mom was so upset as the security guards searched me. She was crying, making a huge scene, which somehow made matters much worse. It was only fifty dollars' worth of makeup. Not that big of a deal, and honestly, she should have been happy I hadn't bothered her for the money. Things were tight enough already, and every time I'd asked her for anything, I got the lecture about needing to be more responsible.

Knox stood there, arms crossed against his chest, trying to calm our mother down. All the while, he looked at me with disappointment. I could still see the piercing gaze now as I lay in bed, staring at the ceiling.

I'd locked myself in my bedroom after we'd got home, refused to have dinner, and told them both to leave me alone. It was finally quiet now, but for the longest time, all I could hear was our mother crying while Knox voiced his disappointment.

I'd heard it all. Neither of them were proud of me. I knew I shouldn't have come on this trip. Tor had warned me. He'd told me they were trying to get me away from him, and he'd apparently been right.

I grabbed my phone off the nightstand, opening up a message to Tor.

Peyton: Miss you.

I stared at the screen of my phone, waiting for a sign that he was there, only there was nothing. Then I remembered he was going to a concert with a bunch of his friends. It was when I opened up one of my social media apps that I learned why he wasn't messaging me back.

Anger flooded me, when my phone pinged with a

message from my best friend Elise. She was at the same concert and sent me a photo, only it wasn't of the band as I hoped it would be. Instead, I blew up the fuzzy photo on my phone. I immediately saw what I didn't want to think was true. It was a picture of Tor and Leela, a girl who hung around his friends. He had her pressed up against the interior brick wall of the building kissing her.

I had a feeling Leela was bad news. I didn't know why I was so upset; it wasn't as if this was the first time I'd caught Tor cheating, and I knew it wouldn't be the last. Yet tears still flooded my eyes. I stared at the picture, hit forward, and sent it directly to Tor with the letters WTF in the message, and hit send.

I got up off the bed and paced my room. The house was quiet. While Mom had gone to bed after she'd calmed down and had dinner, Knox had stayed up for a bit, watching a movie while I surfed on my phone, but he kept at me, asking why I felt the need to shoplift when all I had to do was ask for the money.

He did not know what things had been like. I worked. I picked up extra shifts when I could and helped with the bills and groceries since Mom lost her job. I made a decent wage for part-time while I was in school.

The problem wasn't that I couldn't afford what I wanted to buy. It was Tor. Since he didn't work, he'd started taking money from me. It started with a few dollars here or there and then turned into larger amounts. Just recently, he told me he was in some trouble and needed money, so I cashed in what little savings I had, which left me with nothing, and he was right there the last few paydays taking whatever money I didn't need.

The things I'd taken, I needed, but since I had no way to pay for them and I didn't want to stress Mom out by asking her for the money, I just took them. I wasn't proud of what I'd done. It was wrong on every level, and I knew it, but I felt I had little choice. Tor had bled me dry, and now, after seeing that picture of him and Leela, I knew he didn't love me as he claimed.

I needed to cut him loose, and I knew that by leaving him it would solve so many problems. I'd have money again, after I built things back up. I'd stop having trouble in school because he was the driving force behind why I'd gotten myself kicked out.

I opened the bedroom door a crack and listened. The house was dark. The only light in the hall came from under the door to Knox's room. I could hear him quietly talking, no doubt to his new girlfriend Lorelai, whom we were supposed to meet tonight, until my actions had messed that up as well.

I needed to get out of here.

I grabbed my sweater and tiptoed down the hall

while opening up my maps application. I searched the area for some little bar to go to, finally finding a place called The Tilted Flask within walking distance from here. I checked my emergency spot in my purse to find a twenty tucked inside and figured I could at least buy myself one drink. It would be enough to pull me away from my troubles or allow me some space, because here, I felt like I was suffocating.

MUSIC BLARED inside the bar as the bartender slid a drink in front of me.

"Cheers."

"Cheers." I smiled and clinked my glass against his, taking a sip. "Thanks for the drink."

"No problem, Peyton."

I'd walked into The Tilted Flask and took a seat at the bar. Moments later, Clay Harris walked through the door. I'd met him last summer when Mom and I had come out for their end-of-season celebration. He played with the Dominators for the past five years and was their star goalie. We'd hit it off last summer, and when he walked in tonight, he noticed me immediately, came over, sat down and offered to buy me a drink.

"What brings you in here?" he questioned.

"My brother, my boyfriend…shoplifting… You?"

"Wow, okay, sounds like there may be a story there. I just felt like getting out and having a couple of drinks. Care to tell me what happened?" he asked.

I opened the image on my phone, looked at it, and then placed my phone down on the bar top, showing it to him.

"Two people kissing… I can see why that would upset you." Clay smiled.

"That part doesn't upset me. The guy in the picture is my boyfriend. As you can tell, it's not me he is kissing. Maybe my brother was right when he told me I should end things with him."

Clay chuckled and thanked the bartender as he slid two beers and two shots down in front of us.

"I'd say your brother is probably right on that one. It doesn't appear to me he knows what he has in front of him or what he is giving up," Clay said, looking into my eyes.

I shrugged, not really knowing what to say to that.

Clay picked up his shot and nodded at mine. I picked it up, and he looked at me. "Cheers to breaking up with shitty guys who don't know what they are losing." He clinked his shot glass against mine before we both downed them.

I wiped my mouth and sat back against my chair.

"So, what else?"

"Knox…" I muttered.

Clay chuckled. "Well, there is a bunch I could say about your brother, but I won't. What did he do?"

"Well, I'm not proud of what happened today, just so you know. It's not like I do this stuff all the time. It was the first time that I'd even thought about doing it, but I got caught shoplifting."

Clay nodded, taking a drink of his beer.

"I see. Well, we all do stupid ass shit sometimes. Most of them turn out to be mistakes, which I'm guessing is how you are feeling, but the main thing is we learn from them. What does your brother have to do about that?"

I let out a sigh. "Well, he acted all perfect, forcing me to face security and then the police."

Clay nodded. "Do you think maybe he was trying to help you, not hurt you by doing that?"

I thought for a moment. "Why do you need to make that make so much sense?"

"Well, because if I had a sister who was getting herself into trouble, I'd probably do the same, but not with any ill will behind it. It would be because I love her, and I don't want to see her go down a destructive path." He winked.

I knew deep down that Knox was only trying to do what was right for me. He was trying to be a male role model in my life that I failed to have after my father left. Neither of us had grown up with a father, and I knew Knox wanted me to have a positive male figure in my life.

"Ugh, you're so right."

"Your brother. His bark is worse than his bite," Clay said, leaning over and bumping me with his shoulder. "He sometimes doesn't know how to show it, but he cares."

"I know. You know, at one point he used to be my best friend, someone I could tell anything to, and then suddenly one day that changed. I don't know why it changed, but it did, and it hurts that I can't go to him when I need him."

"Maybe you should try talking to him and not hiding things from him." Clay winked.

Clay signalled to the bartender and held two fingers up. Immediately, the bartender came over and placed two more shots down in front of us.

"Cheers to overprotective brothers," he said, clinking his glass to mine, and we both tipped our heads back, drinking down the shot.

I smiled at Clay, his blue eyes dancing as he looked at me and smiled.

"Now, about this boyfriend…"

"What about him?" I asked, starting to feel the effects of the shots of alcohol.

"Well, what you just showed me didn't even deserve you to message him. It deserves nothing more than for you never to talk to him again. So, when you get home, what are you going to do?" Clay asked.

I sat there, thinking about the image I'd seen, anger and hurt flooding me.

"I think the first thing I'm going to do is end things with him."

"You think, or you know?" he asked, grabbing my phone and opening the picture I'd shown him. He placed it down in front of me and tapped the screen. "Do you think this will ever stop?"

I shook my head, tears clouding my vision.

"No tears. You know the truth. It's better than never knowing," he said, nudging my chin with his thumb.

"That's true," I said, deleting the photo from my phone and shoving it into my pocket.

"You know, I think it's time for another shot. Then I think we should go out on to the dance floor and dance the night away. What do you say?" Clay asked, signalling the bartender again for two more shots.

I RESTED my head against Clay's shoulder as the Uber he'd called drove us back to Knox's place, finally coming to a stop in his driveway.

I heard Clay whisper my name and felt his hand on my thigh, gently squeezing my leg to get my attention.

"Huh?"

"You're home." Clay said quietly.

I blinked, trying to clear the fuzziness from my eyes. I'd had so much fun tonight. We'd talked, we'd danced, and we'd both drank a lot.

"That was fast," I murmured, trying to undo my seatbelt.

"Here, let me," Clay said, leaning forward a bit and undoing my seatbelt. He leaned across me, letting the belt gently go, and met my eyes. He stared at me and then brought his hand up and brushed a strand of hair back that was in my face.

"You know, I never really realized just how pretty you are," he whispered.

His eyes were glass blue against his dark hair, and as he sat there, looking into my eyes with his hand on my cheek, I wanted nothing more than to feel his lips against mine.

Anticipation filled me as he slowly leaned forward and brushed his lips barley against mine.

I pulled back at first, not sure what had just happened, but as I met his eyes, I leaned forward into him, this time my lips brushing against his. Heat flooded my body as he deepened the kiss. Then, as if someone hit him, he pulled back and cleared his throat, looking forward.

"Peyton, I'm…I'm sorry. I shouldn't have done that," he whispered, looking toward the house where we both knew my brother slept.

"Clay, it's okay…" I said, placing my hand on his arm.

"No, it's not. Let's just pretend that this never happened, because honestly, it shouldn't have happened. It was a moment of weakness on my part. I know better."

I frowned, wishing for nothing more than to continue this kiss.

"I won't say anything," I whispered, placing my hand on his.

"Nor will I because we both know we shouldn't. Good night, Peyton. Go on inside. I'll go home and get some rest, knowing that you're home safe."

I was confused more than anything, but I tugged on the door handle and opened the door. Climbing out, I was about to shut the door when I heard Clay call my name. I bent down and looked into the back seat.

"If you need anything, don't be afraid to reach out. I know how your brother can be. I don't mind if you need to talk." He winked, handing me his card. "Good night, Peyton."

"Night, Clay," I whispered and then shut the door.

I wandered up to the front door and slid my key in the lock, then I tiptoed down the hall, careful not to make too much noise as I almost fell over. I entered my bedroom, flopping down on my bed. Minutes later, still dressed, I fell asleep and dreamt of an amazing kiss.

Chapter Two

Peyton - January 2025

I STOPPED my mother's rundown Honda Civic outside the doors of the airport. My brother's plane should have landed about ten minutes ago, I thought as I glanced around, looking for him. I tapped the dash, trying to get the time to come back on the display, but it did little good.

"Stupid crap car," I said to myself as the time flashed for a moment, then the radio cut out.

I glanced up just as Knox walked out of the double doors, a small bag thrown over his shoulder. Moving the car up, I rolled down the passenger-side window and waved.

We'd just seen Knox at Christmas, and while I hadn't wanted to go all the way to Vancouver after what had happened the last time we were there, Mom made me. I'd cleaned up my act a lot since then, hadn't shoplifted since, and thanks to Knox calling me after I'd returned and talking some sense into me, I'd returned to school. It had helped that he'd called and spoken with the administration as well—and had probably been forced to make some outlandish donations to the school for them to allow me back in. I'd been a trouble child, and I knew it.

"It's about time you got here," he said as he climbed into the front seat after throwing his bags in the back seat.

"Me! Hey, buddy, I'm the one on time. You are late." I giggled as I put the car in drive and pulled away from the curb.

"So, things going well?" he asked as he reached behind him for the seat belt.

"Yeah," I said, carefully merging onto the highway.

"School?"

"In class every day, on time, doing all assignments like I promised. I even got a passing mark on my last test."

"That's great. And what about Tor? You still seeing him?"

I knew he was going to ask me about Tor. I'd

promised him I'd end things with him when I left the first time, but I hadn't. Again, he asked me, and I'd promised once again I'd end it after Christmas. I still hadn't ended things with him. I didn't see the need. He wasn't that much of a bad influence in my life, and I'd already made a lot of changes, so instead I'd kept it quiet and given Tor one last chance. I'd taken the things that were bugging me about our relationship and made him make a promise to me not to do them anymore, which he had in some roundabout way.

I knew Knox was going to be disappointed in my decision and, as I looked over at my brother, I told him what he wanted to hear.

"He's gone," I said, swallowing hard.

I glanced over at my brother to see him nod in my direction.

"Good. I'm glad. He was a bad influence." He was quiet for a few minutes and then looked over at me. "Peyton, I'll admit I'm confused about why I'm here. The email Mom sent said I was coming here because she needed some help with you, but now that I know things are fine, or so they seem, I'd like to know why I'm here. You and Mom both know that Lorelai and I are in the middle of planning our wedding, and she likes to have the help from me when I'm home."

I tapped the steering wheel. Yes, I'd emailed Knox using my mother's email. I'd written as if I were her, telling him she needed help with me because I was in some sort of trouble, asking that he come as soon as he could. I knew Knox would do anything for Mom and that he'd be on the first flight to Vermont. I should have just been honest instead, because instead of me, it was Mom I was concerned about, and since I knew he'd do anything for her, there really had been no point in making anything up.

"Okay, don't be angry." I sighed.

I didn't even need to look; I knew Knox was looking at me and that he had a questioning look on his face.

"I emailed you from Mom's account under the guise of her, but for a valid reason."

"Dammit, Peyton. Lorelai and I were supposed to be picking out invitations this weekend and possibly going to look at a few venues."

"I know, it was wrong, but if you'd just let me explain," I said, swallowing hard, suddenly feeling bad that I'd gotten him here under false pretenses. Well, not false; there was a problem. For the first time in a long time, it just didn't pertain to me. I didn't want Knox pissed off at me. I wanted him to give me a chance to explain.

"Okay, explain, because right now I'm wondering if you aren't just up to one of your old tricks. That maybe everything you've just told me is all just bullshit."

"I swear, I'm not up to anything. Everything is going well for me, I promise you that." I sighed.

"Then what is it?"

"I'm worried about Mom," I said, getting right to the point.

I glanced over at Knox to see a concerned look on his face. "Why? What is going on?" he questioned.

Mom had gone on one date with William just before we'd gone to visit Knox a few months ago. It wasn't really anything to even mention when we'd been out there. When we returned, they'd started dating and going out a little more often. I'd often hear them arguing after a date and was almost certain that one night he threatened her.

While we'd been in Vancouver at Christmas, I'd wanted to tell Knox about him, and that I'd sensed there might be some type of abuse going on, but Mom had assured me I was worrying over nothing.

When we'd returned from that trip, things had gotten bad. I feared for my mother's safety, but she continuously made me promise I wouldn't mention anything. I wasn't even sure if Knox knew she was seeing anyone, but lately it seemed things had spun out of control between her and William.

"It's William," I answered.

"Who the fuck is William?" Knox questioned.

Just what I'd thought. He did not know Mom was even seeing anyone, which meant she could be in trouble, because I knew Mom told Knox pretty much everything.

"Mom, didn't want you to know when we were there at Christmas, in case things didn't work out, but William is the man Mom is seeing."

"Uh-huh." Knox grunted as I pulled the car into the driveway of the rental unit Mom and I lived in.

I immediately recognized William's car in the driveway, which meant he was here and chances of things becoming heated were inevitable.

"It looks like you're about to meet him, too. Let me warn you, you're in for a real treat," I said, opening the car door and climbing out.

The moment we climbed out of the car, I could hear him yelling, and I flinched when I heard him call her the name I probably hated more than anything.

"What the fuck?" Knox gritted.

One thing about my brother, he had a temper if provoked. He also had a temper with how others treated any of his family members. He was also a big man, and I knew he could truly hurt someone if he wanted to, and there was no way I'd ever be able to hold him back.

"William is our landlord and a hotshot lawyer out

here, and he has some serious mental health issues. He's a narcissist, a gas lighter, and emotionally abusive," I muttered, which I knew was the exact type of man Knox's father had been, along with mine, which was why I was so afraid for her.

It was then we heard William yell, followed by glass shattering. Knox looked at me, and before I could get a word out, he was already up the stairs and at the door, leaving me standing there with my heart in my throat. He ripped the door open and went inside, raising his voice while I trailed behind him.

William stood in the living room, a look of shock on his face as Knox stood over him, looking down at him.

"Put the fucking vase down now," Knox said in a calm and controlled voice, which surprised me.

Mom looked up at me and then over to where Knox stood, her face contorted in a shocked and surprised but thankful look.

"Who the fuck are you?" William shouted at Knox.

"Your worst fucking nightmare, especially if you don't put the vase down and leave right now." He clenched and unclenched his fists, which I knew meant that if William didn't heed the warning, Knox would no doubt hit him.

"Who's going to make me? You?"

He didn't recognize him. Anyone who watched

hockey knew Knox wasn't someone to mess with. Before he'd started dating Lorelai, Knox had been in a pile of fights and that had only been because of the adrenaline rush during a game, or so he said. I'd seen the damage he'd caused during those games, and I had no clue what he would be capable of with someone who'd hurt or endangered his family.

"Yeah, me. Now, get out."

Mom stood there, tears in her eyes, as William and Knox faced off with one another.

"Knox, please, it's okay," Mom cried, placing her hand on his forearm, trying to pull his attention from William.

"Mom, I don't want to hear it. This jackass is going to leave, and he's going to leave now."

William ignored Knox's warnings and grabbed Mom's forearm roughly, making her wince and scream in pain as he looked her in the eye.

"Reese, tell your friend here to back the fuck off," he growled.

"That's it!" Knox muttered.

I didn't know how things sped up so quickly, but the next thing I knew, Knox had a hold of William. His arm was snaked around his neck as he punched him in the stomach. William released a grunt as Knox dragged him toward the door. The moment he let him go, William fell to the floor, clutching his stomach, breathing rapidly.

"You shouldn't have done that," he said, coughing so hard I feared he might be sick.

"You shouldn't have put your hands on my mother. Now get the fuck out!" Knox shouted.

"Hope you got an excellent lawyer there, kid, 'cause I'm going to sue your fucking ass," William said, struggling to get up off the floor.

"Go ahead, my lawyers eat parasites like you for fucking breakfast," Knox said, getting into his face again.

Knox stood there, staring down at William until he finally backed out the door and took off, climbing into his car. Knox didn't say a word. Instead, he kept his eyes trained on the driveway for a few minutes, making sure William didn't return.

I went over and wrapped my arms around Mom, pulling her in for a hug, making sure she was okay. Once I was certain she was fine, Mom cried. I'd heard her cry almost every night for the past two months, and I couldn't take it anymore. Even though she'd told me repeatedly not to worry about the situation, but each time things escalated. I'd done the only thing I could think of and that was to get my brother involved before William did more than just emotionally hurt her, and it looked like I'd gotten him here just in time.

Knox shut the front door, locking it, and turned toward us both. He was angry. I could see it all over his face. I should have told him what was going on way before now, instead of surprising him the way I had. I'd been wrong to do that.

"Knox, really, it's not as bad as it appeared," Mom cried, rubbing her forearm.

"Not as bad as it appeared? Mom, what the hell. When this was Peyton, you tore her away from the guy!" Knox shouted.

"Well, that was different. This is not the same thing."

"Mom, please tell me you aren't actually defending him?" I questioned, anger growing inside of me.

Knox crossed his arms and began pacing back and forth as we both waited for Mom to answer my question. When she didn't immediately answer me, I looked over at Knox.

"That's it. Pack your stuff," he demanded.

I frowned as I looked over at my half-brother. "What for?" I questioned.

"We're going to Vancouver. I don't want to hear any more. I'm calling the airport, and we are getting on the next flight that leaves tonight." He pulled his phone from his pocket. "We will file a police report here when we get out there, followed by a call to my lawyer."

"Vancouver? Knox, you are being unreasonable, and there is no reason to file a police report," Mom said, looking over at me.

"No Mom, unreasonable is getting a panicked email from you, rushing here thinking Peyton is in trouble and that you are at your wit's end, only to find out that it isn't Peyton in trouble at all. Instead, I find out it's you and that you are involved with yet another crappy guy. Jesus. Didn't you learn from Dad and Peyton's father?"

"Knox, please, let's just sit down. Give me a chance to explain things," Mom pleaded as she looked over at me, a look of disappointment on her face that I'd gone against her wishes.

"There isn't time. I've got to be back in Vancouver for a game tomorrow. Now, go get packed, both of you, while I book our seats and then maybe call my lawyer now, instead of waiting. No doubt I'm gonna need one," he said, running his hand through his hair.

The one thing about my brother that I loved and hated all at the same time was how damn protective he was of his friends and family. I remembered Clay, telling me that very thing that night back in October when I'd run into him in that dingy little bar I'd taken off to the night they had caught me stealing. The night we shared that first kiss. I'd always had a crush on Clay, but I also knew how my brother would react. Hell, he'd made me promise him I'd never get involved with any player on the team, so of course, I could only imagine how he'd have been knowing he'd kissed me.

"I'll help you pack, Mom, and I'll take care of things here while you're gone."

Knox turned and looked in my direction. "No way, you're coming too. If you think I'm leaving you here to deal with that asshole, you're wrong."

"Knox, there is no reason for me to go with you, too."

"No? Are you able to protect yourself from that guy when he comes back in a full-on rage?" Knox questioned.

I was just about to answer him when Mom put her hand on my arm.

"Honey, maybe it will do us both good to get away. Get me away from William, and you could use a break from Tor. Lord knows he's been giving you a lot of trouble lately."

Heat flooded my body. I didn't even need to look; I knew Knox was staring at me, but I lifted my eyes anyway. Sure enough, he stared back at me, his eyes filled with disappointment at my lie. He shook his head.

"Knox—"

"I have nothing to say to you right now," he grunted.

"Peyton?" Mom questioned. I could see the questions in her eyes.

"Fine, I'll come with you, but only for the weekend, Mom."

"Uh-huh," Knox grunted as he turned his attention back to his phone. "I swear if I ever lay eyes on this Tor guy, I'll do to him what I should have done to William tonight," Knox muttered.

"Peyton, honey, plan to stay a little longer than only the weekend, please," Mom said as I led her up the staircase.

I cleared my throat as I made eye contact with Knox. "Mom, you know I have to go to work on Wednesday," I said loud enough for Knox to hear as I followed Mom up the stairs to our rooms to pack, leaving Knox downstairs to book our flight.

WE'D BEEN in Vancouver less than twenty-four hours and already I wished I'd stayed home. I wandered into the living room and flopped down on the couch, pulling out my phone and checking to see if I had any messages. I let out a sigh when I saw no one had tried to contact me.

Mom had gone with Lorelai to the grocery store. They'd asked me if I wanted to join them, but I declined, hoping I'd have the house to myself. Instead, five minutes after they left, Knox came home from practice and went straight to the kitchen where he made himself lunch.

"Why did you lie to me?" he questioned, coming into the living room with a jug of water and a plate of food. He sat across from me, flipping the TV on, going directly to the sports channel.

"Huh?" I questioned, looking up from the message I was sending off to Tor.

"About Tor? Why did you lie to me?" he questioned.

I'd avoided Knox ever since we arrived here. It hadn't been hard. He had to get right to bed because he had practice early this morning, and I figured he'd be gone for most of the day, but he'd come home to unwind before tonight's game.

"I wouldn't say I lied."

"What would you call it then? You told me you ended things with him. You also told me you went back to school, or is that a lie as well?"

"No, school isn't a lie," I said, getting my back up. "I really don't understand why it's any of your business anyway."

"It's my business because it's my money that is

paying your tuition. It was also my money that paid to get your ass back into school after you messed up the last time. So, I'm sorry if I have a vested interest in your schooling and who you are dating, and if you're being treated properly and not messing up your life by getting involved with the wrong people."

"God, you sound like Mom."

"Perhaps you'll listen to me better than you listen to her."

"Whatever." I rolled my eyes and returned my attention to the message I was sending.

"Peyton, how about you pay attention to something other than that bloody phone?"

"What?" I said through clenched teeth, placing the phone down on the arm of the chair.

"How did you feel when you saw how William was treating Mom?" Knox asked, taking a bite of a chicken wrap Lorelai had made him for lunch.

"I didn't like it." I shrugged.

"Were you scared?"

"Yes, I was scared."

Knox nodded, as if he already knew the answer I was going to give him.

"Does Tor treat you that way?"

I swallowed hard. Tor was worse than William in some ways, but I'd never let on about those times. He was degrading and a thief and someone I was completely afraid of, which I knew was the reason I'd given him another chance. I did not know how he'd react if I told him I didn't want to see him anymore.

I barely nodded, but it was a nod, and I knew Knox had seen it.

"Peyton, there are better guys out there. It's better for you to be involved with those who support you and lift you up, instead of surrounding yourself with those that bring you down."

"I wouldn't say he brings me down."

"I would. Is he in school?"

I shook my head. Tor had dropped out of high school after he failed the eleventh grade.

"Does he have a job?"

Again, I shook my head, growing a little more irritated. The last job Tor had he'd been fired from after he told off a customer.

"Does he support you in going to school?"

Tor and I had many fights over me being in school. He wasn't a fan of education and didn't think it was necessary. He always said I could be just like him, since he'd done fine without it. Tor also made it known to me he hated the fact that I worked, even though, thanks to my job, it meant that he had money for his drugs, since he normally took most if not all of what I made.

"Well?"

"Knox, I don't want to talk about this anymore."

"Of course not, because you know I'm right, and you'd never want to admit that. I guess until you tire of being treated worse than the gum on the bottom of my shoe, this is a complete waste of my time and breath."

"You know I'm right," I mimicked, growing even more annoyed at his holier-than-thou attitude.

"Peyton, I'm going to tell you something, and I'm only going to say it once. After this, if you don't get it, you're on your own. Allowing others to dim your light and not let you shine like the star you are only brings you down to their level. Learn it and start surrounding yourself with those who bring you higher."

"Oh what, like you do?"

"Yes, exactly like I do."

"When are you going to get it, Knox? I'm not you."

"Of course you aren't me, but you're not a piece of garbage either, Peyton. You are a smart girl capable of having an amazing career in whatever area you decide. You're also an attractive girl, and if only you'd believe in yourself, it might change some things for you."

"Knox, Tor doesn't bring me down." I sighed.

"Yes, Peyton, he does. Mom thinks he's the reason you ended up being removed from school. It doesn't take a genius to figure out that he was the reason that you were shoplifting, too."

"No, he's not the reason I was shoplifting," I lied, knowing full well he was the reason. At the time, he'd taken every drop of my last six paychecks, aside from what I'd owed to Mom for two of the bills, to pay his pusher for the drugs he'd gotten, leaving me with no choice but to shoplift the things I needed. Mom had been struggling financially after being out of work for a little over two years, so I did what I had to do.

"Believe what you want, but I'm telling you now. I know the truth, Peyton."

"No, you think you know," I said, crossing my arms over my chest.

"Well, William and Tor are the reasons I'm debating moving you and Mom here to Vancouver."

"What?" I questioned, almost horrified at the thought of moving away from Tor and my friends.

"Yep, Lorelai and I have already talked it over, and tonight I plan on bringing it up to Mom."

I watched as Knox shoved the rest of his chicken wrap into his mouth and then sat back in his chair. The more I stared at him, the angrier I got.

"You know, for someone who has a lot to say about people bringing others down, why are you allowing Mother and I to bring you down?" I bit back.

Knox let out a breath and rested his head against the back of the chair.

"Peyton, you aren't people, you're my family.

Mom's going through a rough patch, no doubt because of all the shit you've put her through. You're on a collision course and are about to crash."

My mouth dropped open at what he'd just said. Had he really blamed my mother's problems and toxic relationship on me?

"Stand there looking like that all you want, Peyton. I speak to Mom pretty much every week. I hear what is going on, and I can see how it's affecting her, and I live across the country. I know the shit you've been up to better than you do."

"If you know everything, then you should have known I was lying to you about Tor," I said, a smug smile on my face.

"Trust me, I knew. I'd hoped I'd been wrong. All I try to do for you is to make sure you have the things I didn't while growing up. I want to make the path you choose easier to navigate than it was for me."

"You are such an ass."

"Really?" Knox said, standing up and crossing his arms.

"Yes, really. You, brother… are an ass," I said, walking up to him and poking him in the chest with my forefinger. "God, Tor was right about you."

Knox stared at me. There was no way I was going to win this stare down. The intensity in his eyes was insane, and soon I could feel his tension throughout my entire body.

"Peyton, all I want is to be able to trust you, and for you to know that no matter what, you can always come to me when you're ever in trouble."

I tried to maintain eye contact, but when I heard a key in the door, I swallowed hard and tore my eyes away. Lorelai and Mom walked into the living room, their conversation coming to a complete halt as they saw the two of us standing only a few inches apart.

"Is everything alright?" Mom asked, finally breaking the silence.

"Fine," we both uttered.

"Doesn't look that way," Mom added, coming over to me. She went to place her hand on my shoulder, but I moved out of the way.

"I'm going out," I said, grabbing my phone from the arm of the chair I'd been sitting in before making my way over to the door.

"What do you mean? Lorelai and I got everything to make pizza, just like you asked," she said.

"Great, enjoy," I muttered, slipping my shoes on, not caring about anything.

"Where are you going?" Mom questioned.

I looked over at my brother, who was staring at me, his eyes even more intense now than before.

"Out to find someone else that will bring me down to their level."

"What is that supposed to mean?" Mom cried as she looked at me and then over at Knox. I could see the worry in her eyes and was glad she'd turned away from me.

"See you all later," I muttered and pulled the door shut behind me, closing off this moment in time for at least a little while.

Chapter Three

Clay

I glanced at my watch. Where the hell were Lucas and Knox? I'd been sitting in The Tilted Flask for about half an hour, waiting for the guys. This wasn't our usual hangout. We'd only agreed to come here because our normal hangout, Illusions, was under some major renovation.

I checked my phone for any messages from either of them. There was nothing. In fact, neither of them had even read the reminder message I'd sent a little over an hour ago when I'd pulled into the parking lot.

Figures, I thought to myself.

They were both busy with their lives. Knox and Lorelai were in the middle of planning their wedding, and ever since Lucas surprised us with his marriage announcement to Ella, he'd become unavailable almost every night we were home.

Dylan and I figured that tonight would be a good boys' night, since the girls were supposed to be getting together. Then he dropped the bomb that he couldn't make it. He was still trying to work things out with his father before he and Aurora got married and the baby was born.

I nodded at the bartender to bring me another beer and glanced across the bar. I'd been watching the couple that were sitting down near the end of the bar. Perhaps they weren't even a couple. He appeared to be considerably older than her, hovering around her like flies to a slice of rotten meat, and her body language screamed that she wanted to be left alone.

The more I watched her, the more I noticed how uncomfortable she looked. Even at this distance, I couldn't help but think that she looked familiar to me, like I knew her from somewhere, and for the past ten minutes, I'd been trying to place her. Then she glanced my way. The moment our eyes met, I knew where I'd seen her before.

I swallowed hard, growing more irritated as I

watched this guy paw all over Peyton, Knox's younger sister. What the hell was she doing here?

Maybe it was a good thing Knox wasn't here now, I thought to myself.

As I sat there, continuing to watch them, I realized how pretty she really was. Hell, the last time I'd run into her, I'd slipped and kissed her. It wasn't exactly one of my proudest moments, and while I'd regretted it for a few reasons, I'd not for many others. I'd always found her attractive, and if I hadn't been afraid of having my nuts removed from her brother, I'd have gone in for the kill. The entire situation truly was a double-edged sword.

I glanced across the bar again only to see her staring at me—everything about her, her body language, her eyes were pleading for help.

"Hey, man, thanks for the beer. Could I get one more, please?" I asked the bartender, who'd just placed the bottle down in front of me at the perfect time.

"Sure thing," he said, cracking the other bottle and setting it down in front of me.

"I'm just going to head on over there, but you have my card."

"Sure thing," he said glancing to the opposite side of the bar before moving on to the next patron.

I gathered both bottles, my jacket, and got up off my seat, making my way around the bar. I came up behind Peyton, making sure the guy who was hitting on her saw me coming. He eyed me as I approached them.

"Hey, buddy. Can I help you?" he asked as I stood there making eye contact with him before placing my jacket on the back of her chair.

Peyton looked up at me, her eyes pleading with me for help. I placed my free hand on her shoulder and set both bottles down on the bar in front of her.

"Here you go, darling. Sorry I was late. Couldn't get out of work. You know how it is. Then, of course, traffic was insane," I added.

"Who the fuck are you?" the guy asked, taking on a bit of a defensive stance.

He hadn't seen me sitting across the bar, which only gave me the advantage. I mean, how could he have noticed me? He'd practically been drooling in her lap the entire time I'd been watching them.

"One should ask you that," I said, my voice calm as I bent down and placed a kiss on the top of Peyton's head and gently massaged the back of her neck.

"Is this your fucking boyfriend?" the man asked, looking at her, gripping his beer bottle tight enough his knuckles turned white.

Peyton took hold of my hand that now rested on her shoulder and nodded.

"Fucking sluts…" the man muttered to himself as

he turned around and made his way deeper into the bar.

At least he knew what was good for him, I thought as I took a seat beside Peyton and grabbed one bottle of beer I'd brought over.

"What the hell are you doing here?" I questioned, nodding to the beer I'd placed in front of her.

"Trying to unwind. What about you, Clay?"

"Ah, I see. Well, I was supposed to meet your brother and Lucas here, but it appears I'm on my own. So, I guess you could say I'm here unwinding as well."

"While I can't speak for Lucas, Knox won't be coming, thank goodness. He's at home dealing with my mother."

"Why? What's wrong with Mom?" I questioned, taking a drink.

"Abusive boyfriend."

"Ah, and what about you? How are things from the last time you were here? Did you clean up your act like you promised?"

"Let's just say I somewhat kept my promise, and before you go all high and mighty on me, Knox has already dealt with me, which is why I'm here. So, I don't need another lecture from big brother."

I chuckled. "No lecture, I was just curious. People will do what they want when they want. No skin off my back."

She picked up the beer bottle and clinked it against mine. "At least you get it," she said, taking a mouthful of beer.

"I do, probably better than most. Do you mind if I sit with you for a bit?"

"As long as you're okay with putting up with the other Evans tonight?" she questioned, winking at me.

I chuckled under my breath. "Then I guess lucks on my side. You're the better-looking Evans, anyway." I winked. "So, when did you get into town? Knox didn't mention to anyone that you guys were coming."

"That's because we weren't. Knox came home to deal with this ass that was going to end up killing our mother. He forced me to come out here after he found out through my mother that I was still dealing with Tor."

"Ah, I see. I thought we devised a plan the last time you were here to get you away from him?" I asked, grabbing her beer to see she had about as much as I had left, then signalled to the bartender for two more.

"We did," she said, looking over at me, those beautiful green eyes staring back at me.

"What happened?"

"It wasn't as easy as I thought once I got back and talked to him."

I met her eyes and nodded.

"Let me guess, he made promises to you he'd

change, promised you the world, and has so far delivered on none of them."

She sat there looking over at me with a stunned expression.

"How'd you guess it went something like that?" she asked, helping herself to one of the cold beers the bartender had dropped off, taking a drink.

"Because I have a dick too, Peyton," I said, leaning into her, giving her a nudge with my shoulder. "If it meant keeping some pretty little thing like you attached to my side and in my bed, that would come at my beck and call, no matter how I treated her, I'd tell her what she wanted to hear as well. If I were the same type of guy, that is."

"Does my brother know you treat women that way?"

"No, darlin', because I don't treat women that way."

"Is that so? What's the difference then between you and Tor?"

I couldn't help but chuckle as I took a mouthful of beer.

"Well, the difference is I'm a fucking man. I treat you the way you should be treated— with respect. I don't play games, and I'd never tell you something just because I know it was what you wanted to hear. Guys like Tor don't deserve girls like you—or anyone, for that fact."

Peyton tore her eyes away from me and looked down at the bottle in her hands. She picked at the corner of the label for a few seconds, her hand shaking.

"What do you mean, girls like me?"

"Girls like you—smart, attractive, girls with a future. Guys like him, they aren't going any further than where they are right now, except maybe to jail, and they will hightail it on the first signs of trouble only to pick their next victim. Exactly like the guy you were talking to earlier. The second he laid eyes on me, he placed a nasty label on you and took off looking for his next piece of meat," I said, nodding over toward the corner.

Peyton looked over to see exactly what I meant. The guy who'd been all over her when I approached was already talking with another girl who was feeding out of the palm of his hand. We sat there watching them; he took the drink out of her hand and guided her toward the door, both of them leaving the bar.

"How did you do that?" she asked, looking over at me.

"Do what? Read him?"

She slowly nodded.

"As I told you—"

"You have a dick," she said, meeting my eyes.

She stared at me for a few minutes and then tore her eyes from mine, looking back down at the bottle in her hand, picking at the label again.

"You feel like getting out of here?" I questioned, placing my arm across the back of her chair.

Peyton shrugged. "I don't want to go home just yet. I don't want to listen to my brother go off on my mom, or on me again," she said, looking up at one of the TVs that was playing a hockey game.

"I didn't say get out of here and go home. I asked if you wanted to get out of here, maybe come back to my place. Have you eaten?"

She shook her head as she looked up at me.

"Well, we could order in some food. Watch a movie or the rest of the game." I nodded toward the TV, then turned my attention to her.

She looked up at me. God, she was gorgeous—those beautiful large green eyes, those perfect, full bowed lips. God, I'd love to kiss her again, but I knew there was no way in hell I could or should touch her.

"That sounds fun. Let's go."

I took care of the bill while she threw her coat on, and together we made our way out of the dingy little bar.

THE TV WAS ON, casting a soft glow over my living room. Empty beer bottles and dirty plates sat on the coffee table in front of us. We'd picked up Thai food before coming up to my place, enjoyed the meal as we talked, drank, and watched the game before one thing led to the other.

Peyton now straddled my lap, my fingers combed through her hair as we kissed, my left hand gripping her ass. A soft moan escaped her as she ground her hips against me.

I'd lost track of how we'd gotten to this point. All I knew was that it had to do with all the empty bottles that lay on my living room table, and a brief conversation about the kiss we'd shared in the car the last time she'd been here. Then one little kiss had led to her straddling my lap.

"God, I want more of you." She moaned into my mouth as her lips danced against mine.

I wrapped my arms around her and stood up as she wrapped her legs around my waist, her arms around my neck, sucking my bottom lip between hers.

I carried her down the hall, toward the bedroom, dropping her almost-naked body down on the bed. I wasted no time. I dropped my pants, letting them fall to my feet, and joined her on the bed, unclasping her bra, taking her right nipple into my mouth, swirling my tongue over the hardened nub.

She fisted my hair as I bit down a little, causing her to cry out.

"Not so hard." She giggled as I sucked the other into my mouth while my fingers played with the other.

"Pain is part of the fun, darlin'. Give me five minutes, and you'll be begging me for things to be harder."

I pulled my shirt off over my head, throwing it to the corner of the room, and took hold of her legs, parting them. I lifted one of her legs, resting it on my shoulder, and took a moment to kiss the inside of her ankle, then her knee.

She let out a soft moan as she watched me move to the other leg and repeat the same thing. I slid my hands down her inner thighs, squeezing them, as my thumbs rubbed circles close to her centre.

She closed her eyes and arched her back as I brought my hands around her hips, resting them on her perfect ass. I kissed her lower abdomen, then placed tiny kisses on the tops of her thighs, dragging my tongue to her inner thigh.

"Don't tease." She moaned.

"I love to tease," I whispered, taking a tiny taste of her and giving her nothing more for the moment.

She looked down at me as I placed soft kisses once again on her inner thighs. She wanted more. I could see it in her eyes as I ran my fingers along the tops of her thighs. I watched her as she watched me, pleading with her eyes for more until I could no longer deny her. I gave her what she wanted, this time running my tongue over her clit many times before sucking it between my lips.

"Holy hell," she cried out, fisting my hair.

"You like that?" I questioned, watching her body lift off the bed.

She was about to say something when I repeated the move, watching as her head fell against the pillow and her back arched off the bed. I took that opportunity to take her breasts in my hands and roll her nipples between my fingers, making her moan loudly.

"Oh god..." she cried, breathless. "Do it..."

Before she could get the words out, I repeated that little trick one last time, sucking her clit between my lips again, this time allowing her to build toward her orgasm a little more. Just as she tightened her legs around my head, I stopped, then pushed her legs open, got up on my knees, and reached for a condom. Slipping it on myself, I lined myself up and thrust deep inside of her.

"Oh god..." she moaned, biting her bottom lip as she looked up at me.

I took both her legs, placed each one on my shoulders, and leaned forward, pumping fast and deep inside her. I felt her hands rest on my hips, as most girls did when I took them this way. They figured they could control me, slow me down, but I always proved them wrong.

"Hope you're ready to be taken like you should be," I stated, looking deep into her eyes where the anticipation lay.

I thrust deep into her, over and over, until I felt her tightening, then pulled out, flipping her over onto her stomach.

She was easy to maneuver, being so tiny, as most girls were for me. I gripped her hips, pulling her back so she was on her knees. I lined myself against her and thrust deep inside as she let out another deep moan.

Slowing my pace, I ran my hands over the cheeks of her ass, giving her a light tap.

"You ever had your back door played with gorgeous?" I asked, spreading her cheeks and pressing my thumb on the tight button.

She let out a loud moan, then pulled herself forward.

"No." She moaned into the mattress.

Slowing my pace, I continued thrusting into her,

then gripped her hip and pulled her back against me, where I spread her cheeks again.

"I think I'd like to take that one day," I whispered, pressing my finger against that tight little hole, feeling her tense at the idea. "Not to worry, though, not tonight. Tonight, it's just about this pussy. My pussy," I said quietly, burying myself deeper into her.

Gripping her hips tight, I thrust into her, feeling her clench around me while I continued my pace, going as deep as I could, full strokes, bottoming out with each thrust. Her moans filled the room, getting louder and louder the closer she got.

As her pussy tightened around me, she backed up against me, keeping me deep inside her as she came. I could feel myself getting closer as she throbbed around me, combined with the sounds of her moans. Calling my name made my climax come faster than normal. The base of my spine tightened, the room grew dark, and one small move from her, I spilled into her.

Chapter 4

Peyton

WHAT THE HELL *did we do last night?*

THAT WAS the only question that was running through my mind as I watched Clay Harris sleeping beside me. Panic filled me the moment I'd looked over and saw him. I could pretend nothing had happened all I wanted, but the truth was I knew exactly what we'd done last night, because I was sore as hell.

I rolled over and slipped from the bed, my body aching in protest from the number of times we'd had sex through the night and all the positions he'd put me in.

I glanced at the clock on the bedside table; it was close to six thirty, I needed to get the hell out of here. It was Sunday, which meant Knox didn't have practice, and I knew if I walked through the door after he and Lorelai were up, they'd bombard me with questions. Questions I knew I wouldn't want to answer.

I tiptoed across the room, grabbing my bra and panties from the floor before slipping out into the hall, closing the door to his room. I made my way to the living room where our little party for two had started and slipped into my pants and shirt. Putting my socks on, I slipped my feet into my shoes, grabbed my purse, and unlocked his door, slipping into the hallway.

I leaned up against the cool wall and took a breath. My heart was beating wildly. What the hell had we done? Kissing him had been one thing, but I'd just slept with one of Knox's teammates, one of his good friends. I was sure I was going to hell. There was no doubt.

Knox would hate me, especially after he'd made me swear to him after the Ryan disaster that I'd never get involved with one of his friends again. I'd kept my promise until now. I blew out a breath and gathered my thoughts, composing myself. There was no way I could break down now. I needed to remain calm and collected and get my ass home to my room, where I could shed all the tears I wanted.

When I heard the click of a door from down the hall, I quickly pushed myself off the wall and took off toward the elevator, hitting the button to go down. Thankfully, no one joined me. I wanted to be alone with my worry and thoughts.

When the door opened in the main lobby, I exited the elevator and, with my head down, searched my purse for my phone, praying I hadn't left it upstairs. Still digging in my purse, I glanced up in time to see a large frame coming right at me. Without enough time to step out of the way, I ran right into someone, almost knocking me onto the floor.

"Oh god," I cried.

"Peyton?" I heard a deep voice question.

I blinked hard and then met my brother's eyes.

"Knox? What…what are you doing here?" I questioned, swallowing hard as panic boiled inside of me.

"I have a breakfast meeting over at Lavish Mornings with some rep from some skin care company," my brother said, checking his watch.

"Skin care company?" I questioned.

Knox nodded. "Yeah, just an opportunity to be the face of a man's skin care line."

"At six thirty in the morning?" I questioned. "Don't you people sleep?"

"Yes, Peyton, at six thirty in the morning," he said, getting irritated.

"On a Sunday?" I cried.

"Yes, even on a Sunday, and it's for seven fifteen, but I like to make sure I'm early, in case they get here early. It shows that I am eager to hear what they have to say and that I'm interested."

"Well, good luck," I said, waving at him, figuring it might be the best time to run away while he's preoccupied. It would give him less of a chance to ask me questions and more time for me to come up with a story. I'd just about escaped when I heard him clear his throat.

"Wait, what are you doing here? You should be at home in bed," he said, a curious look on his face.

My body heated as even more panic filled me. I should have run when I had the chance, but instead I was now trying to come up with a reason I was leaving Clay Harris's building early in the morning. Knox, of course, would know he lived here.

I swallowed hard, seeing two women come walking in from the road in workout gear, laughing and giggling as they made their way to the elevator.

"Ah, you're wondering why I didn't come home last night, right? Well, funny thing..." I said, laughing nervously. "See, I ran into an old friend last night. We had a few drinks and then we came to her place, here, in this very building. We had a few more drinks, some food, and then I crashed on her couch instead of getting a cab to take me back to your place."

It was sort of the truth, and he'd have to at least be proud I hadn't taken a cab home in that sort of state.

"You could have called me. I'd have come and gotten you," he said.

"I know, but seriously, I was so drunk I really didn't think. I just wanted to sleep. I mean, we'd had a ton of wine, and well, it was just easier. I even passed out while we were watching a movie. She just left me on the couch."

"Uh-huh," he said, giving me a scrutinizing glance.

I stood there, fidgeting with the zipper on my jacket. I couldn't tell if he'd bought my story or not, but I hoped he had.

"How's Mom?" I asked, wanting to take the focus off me.

"Fine. I think Lorelai and I finally got through to her last night. She's going to call William once I get home and tell him they are through. I know she was worried about you, after the way you left last night."

"I keep telling her she doesn't need to worry about me. Yet, I'm thankful that she's taking control of her situation," I said.

"Yeah, I'm glad we finally got through to her, which now we just need to get through to you, but that is a conversation that we'll have later. I don't have time to get into things with you right now."

I jumped when I felt a hand on my shoulder and glanced up at Knox to see he was smiling.

"Hey, man! What the hell you doing up this early on our day off?" Knox asked.

I whipped around to see Clay standing there.

"Hey!" Clay greeted. "Peyton? What are you doing here?" he questioned. "Heading to breakfast with this dopey brother of yours?"

I looked at him, my stomach in my throat as he waited for my response.

"Didn't expect to see either of you here this morning," Clay added when I said nothing.

"No breakfast. I'm just heading home. Spent the night with an old friend."

Clay smirked in my direction with a bullshit-eating grin. It seemed he was enjoying watching me in discomfort. At least that was the look that was written all over his face. I could only imagine what would happen if Knox caught on.

"I'm here for a breakfast meeting," Knox added.

"Right! You got breakfast with that rep today, right?"

"Yep, which I got to get going. As much as I'm skeptical of being the face for a skin care line, it may be good for my career."

"Good luck, man. Anyway, I've got to get going as well. I'm heading to the gym. Who did you say you visited, Peyton? Perhaps I know her. I live here, you know."

I didn't think it was possible to feel more uncomfortable than I already did, but here we were. I felt like I had an angel on one shoulder and the devil on the other.

"Oh, I doubt you know her. She just moved in." I shrugged.

"Not much goes on in this building that I'm not aware of. I'm good friends with the door guy, plus, I'm always on the lookout for a hot girl to date, or maybe take home for the night," he added, winking at me.

I swallowed hard as he met my eyes. I needed to get the hell out of here before Knox caught on to the game Clay was playing, at least the game I thought he was playing.

"You should tell him. Clay knows many people in the building."

"He won't know her," I insisted, becoming annoyed with how persistent my brother was being and the smug look on Clay's face.

"Whatever, Peyton. Look, I've got to go, I'm late. See you both later?"

"Yep, see you at practice tomorrow," Clay added.

Knox nodded and took off toward the restaurant,

while I stood there, staring at Clay for a moment. It was a surprise that Knox hadn't picked up the look on his face.

"Lying to your brother," Clay said, shaking his head, still wearing that cocky smile that I'd always found so attractive.

"Not lying, just omitting some of the truth is all." I added, "I spent the night here. That much is true."

"That's true. Didn't want to tell him you were screaming my name all night?" he asked, placing his hand on my lower back and guiding me toward the door.

"What are you doing?" I questioned.

"Do you want Knox to see us standing here talking?" he asked. "Or do you want him to think you went home and I went to the gym? I mean, if you want questions, I'm sure we can make it happen."

"No, I don't want questions," I answered, swallowing hard as we continued making our way through the lobby. "I don't think you want them either."

"Not really. Now, care to tell me why you ran off this morning?"

I shrugged; did I dare tell him it was because I'd flipped out over what had happened between us?

"Don't you dare tell me it's because you didn't enjoy yourself last night, because I have the marks on my back that beg to differ," he whispered as he pushed the door open and allowed me to go through.

Heat flooded my body as the memory of last night flooded my mind. I'd never say something like that, last night had been the best sexual experience of my life.

"I've got to go."

"It's alright, Peyton. We're in the clear, you can talk with me." Clay added.

"It's good we're in the clear, but I really need to go." I said, heading off toward the bus stop. "See you sometime soon."

I took off down the sidewalk toward the bus stop.

Chapter 5

Clay - Tuesday

PAIN SEARED through me as my body slammed against the boards. It took me a minute to realize what had happened, and then I saw Lucas shake his head and laugh as he skated away from me, fist-bumping Dylan.

"Fucker!" I shouted.

Where the hell had he come from? I shook off the hit and skated after him, deciding to exit the ice instead and sit down.

I grabbed my water bottle as sweat dripped down my face and squirted some into my mouth. The boys and I were just blowing off steam after practice; I knew that, but my mind was on other things, and I wasn't really paying much attention to anything other than the thoughts floating through my mind. That was why I hadn't seen Clark coming toward me.

"What the fuck was that, Harris?" Lucas asked, coming off the ice, to sit beside me, joined by Dylan and our two newest players, Levi and Colton.

"I don't know. I'm asking myself the same question," I said, reaching for my towel and wiping away the sweat that was now stinging my eyes.

"You should be. You never take hits like that, and normally you can see out the back of your head most games. Yet today it seems you couldn't see what's right in front of you."

"I'm a fucking goalie. I should hope the hell I don't take hits like that, otherwise the net is unprotected." I chuckled, taking a swing at Lucas and missing him.

Lucas smacked me in the back of the head and chuckled. "What the fuck is up with you tonight?"

"Guess you could say I'm feeling a little off." I shrugged.

"You're off alright. You were off Sunday night's game too, and you weren't much better yesterday."

"What are you saying?" I questioned.

"I'm saying you better smarten up before the next game," Colton added.

The last thing I needed was to hear from the new

troublemaker of the team that I needed to smarten up. He'd been here three weeks and had had more issues in that short of time than I'd had since joining the team five years ago.

"He'll be fine," Lucas added. "We're all entitled to our bad days."

As if on cue, the lights in the arena went off.

"Guess that means it's time for us to end the night anyway," Dylan said, grabbing his stuff while the rest of us did the same and headed down toward the locker room.

The moment we were in the locker room, Lucas turned on the radio and we all headed for the showers.

"Who's up for dinner?" Dylan questioned, looking at the five of us as we dried and dressed.

"Fuck, I'm starved," Levi and Colton said at the same time.

"Me too. What do you say we head out for some pizza and wings at The Tilted Flask? They have amazing food there," Lucas said, more to Levi and Colton than Dylan and me.

As the memory of Saturday night filled my mind, I immediately jumped up. I couldn't go back to that place tonight.

"Anywhere but that place," I muttered under my breath, swallowing hard as everyone turned and looked at me.

"You love their food. At least you used to until you got spoiled over at Illusions." Dylan chuckled, looking over at me.

"Yeah, isn't that the place you'd wanted to go to the other night?" Colton questioned.

Everyone turned and looked at me, and it was then I realized they'd heard me.

"Well, I've ah, heard through the grapevine their food's gone way downhill. What about The Rusty Anchor?" I said, proud of my quick thinking.

"The Rusty Anchor?" Both Lucas and Dylan said in unison.

It hadn't been the greatest choice off the top of my head. The Rusty Anchor was fan central for us. They were one of the only pubs in town that prided themselves on being Dominator Central for fans. We'd done our best to avoid the place, unless we were forced to make a public appearance. That was why we always went to Illusions when we went out. Not that we went out a lot, but when we did, we liked to remain somewhat anonymous. Illusions gave us that opportunity.

I nodded, praying that if they agreed that tonight no one would recognize us. That was why Illusions was great. We had access to the private rooms, where we could kick back and hang out without worry, but until renovations were done, we'd have to settle with what options we had.

"You're so fucking lucky Knox isn't here right now," Dylan said, slipping his hat on backwards.

"I know." I chuckled.

Knox hated attention, as we all did, and I knew there would be no way he'd ever set foot in there, unless perhaps Lorelai was stuck inside and the building was on fire, but I severely had my doubts he'd go in there even at that point. If he were here, we'd be having food at The Tilted Flask, and I'd have to hide the fact that I'd been there only two nights earlier with his sister.

"I don't give a shit where we go, as long as they have food," Colton added, grabbing his jacket and throwing on his hat. "Let's go."

LUCK WAS on our side tonight, or I guess I should say mine, because the bar was practically empty. We sat in a booth in the back, a half-eaten tray of nachos in the centre of the table when a tray of wings and a pepperoni and mushroom pizza were placed down in front of us.

"Fabulous," Colton said, grabbing a slice of pizza and holding up his glass, asking for another beer.

"Anyone else want another?" the server questioned, smiling.

The rest of us nodded, and just as we were about to dig into the pizza, she cleared her throat and looked at me, an unsettled look on her face.

"I hate to ask, but would it be possible to get a picture of you guys? I mean, for the wall, of course. Our patrons will die knowing you were here, and they'll never believe me without proof," she nervously asked as she pulled her phone from her apron.

I glanced over at the rest of the guys and saw a slight nod from them.

"Sure thing," I answered. "As long as you won't post the picture on social media now or ever."

"Oh no, I wouldn't do that. We, um, we've been told by the owner if ever any of the players from the team were to come in here and we did anything like that we'd lose our job."

"We don't want that now, do we?" I said, winking in her direction, feeling a lot better knowing we would not get mobbed.

The five of us posed for the picture and then dug into the food in front of us while she went and got us more drinks.

"Knox is missing out," Lucas said, adding some nachos to the top of his pizza.

I shook my head as I watched him take a bite of the odd combination, nachos falling all over his shirt.

"Where is he, anyway? Wedding planning?" I questioned.

"Nope. Aurora and Ella are working with Lorelai tonight on some things while Knox takes Peyton back to the airport," Dylan answered.

The second Dylan said Peyton's name, the beer in my mouth hit the back of my throat, causing me to choke.

"You alright?" Dylan questioned, looking at me with a worried expression as I continued to cough.

"Yeah," I finally said, clearing my throat. "Beer hit the back of my throat, I guess."

"As long as you're good."

"Fine," I added, taking another drink.

"Anyway, that's why Knox didn't hang around after practice. He had to take Peyton back to the airport. I guess he didn't want to take her. He mentioned to me he's sure he caught her in a lie this weekend."

"Oh?" I questioned, wanting to know a little more information before I panicked.

"Yeah, I guess it was the morning he ran into her in the lobby of your building."

"Oh yes, I ran into them there as well. Knox was there for that skin care rep, and apparently, she'd spent the night with an old girlfriend."

"Yeah, well, Knox say's it's bullshit. He's sure she was there with some guy and he as much as told her that. He also told her that until she told him the truth, he wouldn't take her to the airport. I guess they had another major blowout before practice, hence his shitty mood. I guess it was a mess. Then their mother got involved and basically forced Knox to take her."

"So, then his mother left as well?" I questioned.

"No, just Peyton. His mother is staying for a bit, helping Lorelai with some things for the wedding."

My mind flew to Peyton and the memory of Saturday night while the guys sat there listening to Dylan. She'd acted odd when she left me after running into her brother, which I guess, given the circumstances, I couldn't blame. I'd figured she'd mellow out once she got home, but from the sounds of things, it hadn't gone that way.

It had been a mindless mistake on my part, going after her once she left. I'd forgotten that Knox was supposed to be there for breakfast with that rep. All I'd wanted to do was talk to her, make sure things were okay. I was certain she was going to have difficulty dealing with what happened between us, and I wanted her to know I was there for her, which was why I'd given her my number.

I'd played it as cool as I could with Knox standing there, even though I knew my cocky side was coming out every time I looked at her. I'd been lucky not to have given anything away. I probably wouldn't look as good as I did right now if he picked up on anything, but he'd been preoccupied with his upcoming meeting.

She looked so stressed, so uncomfortable as she fumbled with her story about why she'd been in my building. Those full cheeks of hers were so flushed I couldn't help but want to take her right back upstairs and make another set of her cheeks match. I could only imagine how wildly her heart was beating as she looked up at her brother, praying he bought her story. It was probably beating just as quickly as it had the night before while she'd been bent over in front of me as I ran my finger over that tight little hole and confessed I wanted to take that part of her as well.

Once Knox rushed off, I followed her outside, hoping to speak to her. I really wanted to apologize for allowing anything to go on between us, even though deep down I'd loved every single minute of it. I may have loved it, but I'd slipped again, but before I could talk to her, she rushed off.

"What about you?" Lucas questioned, looking me straight in the eye.

"Huh?"

"Are you sitting at this table? Jesus, what are your plans for summer?" Lucas asked, clearly annoyed with me. "We've only been talking about it for the last half hour."

"Haven't given it a lot of thought, to be honest. Since I don't have any family, I guess I'll go wherever you asses invite me, otherwise I'll be spending most nights by myself until practice starts up." I shrugged.

Colton and Levi both looked my way, questions about my comment on their lips, but before they could ask, I stopped them both.

"Story for another time, guys," I added, grabbing another slice of pizza.

"Fair enough. We don't want to pry," Levi added, and Colton agreed.

"It wouldn't be prying…Clay will tell you when he is ready," Dylan added.

My personal life had been kept out of the public, thanks to Pamela and her team. I knew it was one aspect of my life that most everyone was curious about, but it was also something I hated sharing, and for good reason. Lucas, Dylan and Knox knew, as did Phil, Lorelai's brother, but I'd sworn them all to secrecy, and so far, they'd all kept their word—something I was grateful for.

It was weird sitting here with the two new guys, but it was fitting. Everything else felt off, so it was a perfect time for them to join us. I'd need new guys to hang around once Knox found out what had happened between his sister and me. It would only be a matter of time.

We continued eating, and soon, the five of us were all discussing our upcoming game and what our chances were that we'd make the playoffs this year. It was a welcome distraction from everything else.

Chapter 6

Peyton

THE CAB PULLED up in front of the townhouse I shared with my mother. I pulled some money from my purse from the money Knox had given me when he'd dropped me off and I paid the cab driver. Thanking him, I carried my bags up to the door and let myself into the dark house.

It was weird being here without Mom. She'd decided to stay in Vancouver with Knox and Lorelai for a while. Well, they'd insisted she stay, just like they had with me. I'd fought them though because I had to work, but I was glad Mom had stayed. The last thing I wanted was for her to come back here and get involved with William again, especially right now. I figured he'd be hanging around waiting for her like some bird of prey, and it honestly surprised me I didn't find him camped out in the driveway waiting for her return.

I grabbed the mail as I entered the house, flipped the lights on, and slipped out of my coat. I locked the front door and then glanced down the hall toward the dark kitchen. The house was so quiet, something I didn't normally think about when Mom was here.

I grabbed the mail from where I'd placed it while hanging up my coat and went into the kitchen, flipping the lights on there. I grabbed a mug and teabag from the cupboard and turned the kettle on. While I waited for it to boil, I flipped through the mail, separating everything into piles.

Once I'd gone through everything, I saw I had three letters, Mom had five bills, and then there was a pile of what I'd deemed garbage mail that sat higher than them all. Each envelope in the junk mail pile had Mom's name written on the outside, all in William's handwriting.

I quickly opened the cupboard where we kept the garbage bin and deposited the pile of envelopes and all their contents into the bin without opening one of them just in time for the kettle to boil.

After pouring my tea, I carried my mug into the living room, turned the TV on, and then started tidying up the room. We'd left in such a hurry the night Knox arrived, that we'd not had time to straighten up. I folded the blankets that were on the couch and started neatly stacking them on the end when I heard a knock on the door.

Irritation flooded me. I didn't feel like visitors. I took a sip of tea before heading to the door. I was certain it would be William. So sure, I'd have put money on it. It appeared he'd been by every day we'd been gone to drop off an envelope, and now that the lights were on inside the place, he'd knock instead.

Without checking to see who it was, I opened the door and was about to tell him to get lost when I looked up and saw Tor standing there, leaning against the house wearing his dirty, worn, and ripped leather jacket and his usual dirty jeans. It appeared he hadn't even showered in a couple of days. His hair was such a mess. As I looked at him, I wondered what the hell had I ever seen in him?

"Tor? What are you—"

"We need to talk," he said, not giving me a chance to finish.

"We have nothing to talk about," I said, shutting the door, but before I could, he stopped it with his hand.

I tried to shove it closed, but he overpowered me like always and pushed his way into the house, first looking into the living room to see if anyone was here with me, then glancing down the hall to the kitchen.

"You here alone?" he asked.

Without thinking, I nodded. "What do you want?" I questioned, crossing my arms in front of my chest.

"Where the hell have you been?" he demanded.

It was at that moment, right there, the tone of his voice, his body language, that things changed for me. Well, perhaps it was Saturday night as I sat in the bar talking with Clay, and after we'd left, that had changed things. Regardless, until that point, the way Tor treated me had been fine. Now it wasn't. I couldn't believe that only a couple of months ago, I'd practically run back into Tor's arms on his stupid, empty promises.

When I'd returned the last time, we'd worked things out, I'd talked to him about the cheating, his abusive words, and how things needed to change. I'd talked to him about not being able to support his drug habit anymore, and he'd promised me he'd change. So, I decided that I'd give him a second chance to see where our relationship could lead.

Of course, he'd treated me no differently than he ever had. Demanding to know where I was every moment of every day, dragging me deeper into trouble with his actions, and dragging me deeper into believing how he treated me was how I was supposed to be treated.

Also, in true Tor fashion, he'd done nothing but cheat and cheat again, each time making me feel like some object that didn't have a choice in the matter.

I'd always chose the troubled men, and it seemed to follow me everywhere I went, even to Vancouver. That was what I learned that night in The Tilted Flask. In my mind, there was nothing wrong with him or the way he was treating me at first, until Clay pointed out the obvious. I was now beginning to wonder if maybe I wasn't the problem here, and because that kind of treatment was what I knew, it was what I was comfortable around.

That night in Vancouver, the guy who'd hit on me had made me feel so uncomfortable and dirty. He'd been whispering all the things he'd do to me if I'd let him, and if I hadn't recognized Clay at the bar, and he hadn't come over to see if I was okay… I shuddered to think about what would have happened.

"Are you going to answer me or just stand there with that stupid look on your face?" Tor demanded.

"Does it really matter where I've been?" I questioned, keeping my back straight.

"If it didn't matter, I would ask. Now where the fuck were you?"

I could see the anger in his eyes, but for the first time, I wasn't afraid. After watching my mother with William, and now seeing Tor's reaction, I knew they were the same, and that in a matter of weeks I could be in the same situation as my mother if I didn't take control of the situation now. If that type of relationship wasn't okay for her, then why was I settling for it?

"I went away for a bit." I shrugged, determined not to be afraid of him any longer.

"You went away for a bit," he mimicked, his steely grey eyes piercing into me.

"Yes, Mom and I went to Vancouver to visit Knox."

"Ah, yes, your rich hockey player, brother. Get any money?" he questioned.

I'd made the mistake the last time of telling Tor about the money Knox had given me to get myself settled in school once they'd reinstated me. Instead of taking that money he'd given and getting the books I needed for my return to school, I'd made the mistake of telling Tor and he'd convinced me to give it to him. He'd spent every dime on alcohol and drugs, which had forced me to lie to my brother again. Instead, I'd had to scrape up some money from my part-time job and bought one textbook instead. For the rest of my courses, I used outdated books that I'd been able to get in the library.

"No money," I said, eyeing my purse that lay on the hall table.

His eyes followed mine and landed on my bag,

which he immediately walked over to and picked up. He looked from me to the purse and smiled.

My heart raced as he opened the zipper and pulled out my wallet where I'd left the five grand Knox had given me to pay up our rent for at least another month, and to take care of the overdue bills we had. I was supposed to get some food, and then the rest was to be put in the bank.

I reached out to take my wallet from him, but he raised it above his head out of my reach.

"You lying to me?" he questioned, staring down into my face.

I swallowed hard, feeling intimidated. "No, I-I'm not," I stuttered.

"Then you won't care if I open it and look inside," he said, bringing my wallet down, watching me as he opened the zipper.

I closed my eyes, knowing full well the first thing he was going to see was the money Knox had given me and, sure enough, he stopped, his eyes meeting mine with anger.

"Didn't give you money? It sure looks like big brother gave you money to me," he said, pulling out the stack of bills then dropping my wallet to the floor. He fanned the crisp bills out in his hand.

"Tor, give it back to me," I said, raising my voice.

He stood there, looking down at the bills in his

hand and shaking his head. "There has to be close to three grand here."

"Five," I said, trying to grab the money again, almost succeeding.

"Sweet!" he said, folding the bills and shoving them deep into his pocket.

"Tor, I need that money."

"So do I, sweet cheeks, so do I," he said, pushing his way into the kitchen.

I followed him, my stomach rolling at the fact he had just taken the money from me. "We need to talk, Tor," I said, "I need that money. It's to pay rent and bills."

"Guess what? I have rent and bills that need to be paid as well. I've also got to pay Jimmy, or otherwise your boyfriend will have no teeth and two black eyes."

Anger flooded me. "You aren't my boyfriend," I said, crossing my arms once again in front of me, hoping that it would comfort me enough to stop shaking.

Tor opened the fridge, grabbing a can of cola. He turned to me and met my eyes, cracking open the can, and took a long swig. "Fuck you, I'm not."

I could feel my insides shake. Anxiety, worry, and fear built inside of me as he studied me, making me feel like I could be sick.

"You're not. When I came back the last time, we

agreed to see how things worked out. You committed to me. You told me you were finished messing around and wanted something serious. You've done the exact opposite, so I'm ending it. We're finished. You've had your chance."

"Pumpkin, I certainly didn't commit to any of that."

"You did too," I cried.

"I didn't. Perhaps I was drunk or high, one of the two, when I did it then." He chuckled, then took another swig, emptying the can of cola.

I stared at him, anger flowing through me at an alarming rate. "You need to leave, and you need to leave now. First, you're giving me the money back."

I was clenching my teeth so hard I thought they were going to crack.

"Fuck that I do. Nope, the cash stays right where it is," he said, smiling smugly as he patted his front pocket.

"Get out. I'm not dealing with your bullshit anymore. You've stepped out on me many times. I deserve more than this," I said, standing my ground for what was the first time in my life.

"I'll get out when I'm damn good and ready," he said, opening the freezer and pulling out a frozen dinner. He was about to open the box when I screamed.

"GET OUT NOW!"

I screamed so loud he dropped the dinner to the floor, and when he spun around, I could see the shock in his eyes, which was quickly replaced with anger.

"Don't you ever raise your voice to me," he said, taking a step toward me, a crazed look in his eyes.

God, I wished I'd kept my word to my brother the last time I'd returned. I should have dumped him then, but in my own true fashion, because I hadn't, things were once again way out of control. I reached for the phone and held the receiver up to my ear.

"What you going to do, call your big hockey player brother?" Tor said, pretending to shake.

"The police, Tor, I'm calling the police, unless you get the hell out."

"Go ahead, call 'em. When they get here, they'll charge your ass for making a phony phone call," he said, moving toward the back door. "Don't call me when you need something. And I'm taking the money," he added, opening the back door.

"Take the money, go ahead!" I screamed. "Just get out."

The back door slammed so hard the glass rattled. I stood there, staring after him, and then I finally ran to the door, locking it and pulling the blind, then I ran to the front door and locked it as well.

Once I knew I was safe, I slid down the door and

collapsed on the floor, my body shaking at what had just happened. I pulled my legs up to my chest and wrapped my arms around them, dropping my head to my knees, sobbing. I'd never thought I'd have it in me to stand up for myself, but I'd done it.

Sobs racked my body as I sat there, then fear crept into me. Knox had been right. I did not know how to protect myself. What if he came back? With Mom gone, and no idea of when she was going to return, I was alone here. Without the money Knox had given me, I had no way to pay the rent or the past due bills, so we'd be homeless soon.

Soon, Tor wouldn't be my biggest problem. William would be my next problem. That, and needing to find a new place for us. All of that combined with explaining to my brother what had happened to the money he'd given me. I felt sick.

TWO WEEKS Later

I PLACED the frozen dinner in the microwave and set the timer, then pulled a soda from the fridge and was about to sit down at the table when I heard a knock on the door. I glanced down the hallway to see if I could make out who it was. All I could see was a dark figure in the window.

I took a deep breath and made my way down the hall, praying it wasn't Tor. I didn't need a repeat of what had happened.

I pulled the door open to see William standing there. My heart sank as he leaned against the doorframe, a creepy smile on his face. I'd purposely been avoiding contacting him because I didn't have the money to pay him.

"Well, well, well. It's about time. You realize you guys are almost three weeks behind on your rent?" he said, pushing his way into the house.

The fact I'd been able to avoid him since I'd been back had been the only good thing that had happened since I'd returned. I'd ignored the phone calls and the text messages from his office and kept the lights off at night in case he'd driven by. It was only when he'd messaged my mother that I'd received a call from her, wondering why I hadn't already paid our rent with the money Knox had given me. In a panic, I'd made up something about working a lot and told her not to worry, that I'd take care of it.

"I know, William. Mom isn't here."

"Yep, I know. She's up there with that son of hers,

the one who's got an immense surprise coming to him once my partner at the firm finishes drafting up the letter, I'm having him write."

I swallowed hard, knowing William wasn't lying. If he was anything at all, he was a snake in the grass, and when he figured he might be able to get money from someone, he'd do whatever it took to make sure it paid off. Unlucky for him, Knox had already had a meeting with his lawyers and William was the one with the surprise coming.

"Regardless of where your mother is, your rent is still due there, sweet cheeks."

My skin crawled each time he called me that.

"Yes, and I've got the money, but it's at the bank. I'll have to see if I can get there before the weekend." I shrugged.

He looked me in the eye, then shook his head.

"Enough of the games, Peyton. Give me my money," he said, taking a step closer to me.

"I told you; I'll get it."

"Then while you're there, get next month's too. I'll be back on Friday to collect."

"Saturday," I answered just as he turned around to leave.

He stopped, glanced over his shoulder at me, and chuckled. "You think I'm playing games? I'll have the two of you booted out of here."

"I know you aren't playing, William. I'll have it on Saturday. I promise."

"Saturday, nine in the morning. Not a minute later," he said, and then turned and left the house, slamming the door behind him.

I stood there, tears filling my eyes until the entire room was blurry. My stomach rolled. Maybe I should just be like Mom, I thought. We talked the other night. She'd expressed an interest in changing her life and had wanted me to consider the same. She told me, for now, only to pay one month's rent, and by that time she'd have her answer whether she was going to move to Vancouver to be closer to Lorelai and Knox or return to Vermont. Maybe, just maybe, I should do the same, I thought and made my way back to the kitchen just in time for the microwave to go off.

Chapter 7

Clay

THERE WAS LESS than a minute to go. I stood in the net, sweat dripping down my body as I watched the opposing team slay their way through the boys, heading straight for me. I'd lost the time and prayed I could either stop the puck when they shot it toward the net, or the buzzer beat them to it. Almost immediately after the opposing player shot the puck toward me, I blocked, and the buzzer sounded. I did not know if I'd stopped the puck from going in the net or not until the arena broke out in cheer.

Winning the game on home ground was always unlike any other.

The sirens went off and the boys all came skating over, piling into me, while the crowd continued cheering.

We were one step closer to securing our spot in the playoffs once again.

"Killer save!" Dylan yelled.

"Amazing, I thought we were done," Colton said, fist-bumping me.

Lucas, Knox and Levi bro hugged me, and then I met with the rest of the team as they came out on the ice. Once we'd done the end of the game rounds, we headed back to exit the ice, but first we stopped to sign a few things for some fans.

"We should go out and celebrate," Levi said as we made our way to the locker room.

"I'm down," Colton agreed.

"I'll check and see if Aurora's okay with me going," Dylan said. "You guys going to come out with us? Illusions just announced their grand reopening tonight."

"Yeah, you know, if we are going there, then I think I will go," Knox said, looking at me, waiting for my reply.

The last thing I felt like doing was going out to celebrate our win. It hadn't helped that I hadn't been able to get my mind off Peyton since she'd left the other night. The entire situation was eating at me on so many levels. I'd barely been able to look Knox in the face. I wanted to confess everything, take my beating and be done with the entire situation. Then tonight, right before we were going on the ice, Peyton had texted asking if we could talk. I made sure I was alone when I quickly responded, constantly checking over my shoulder as I told her I'd message her after the game once I was home.

"Well? What do you say?" Knox questioned.

THE MUSIC WAS POUNDING, so was my head as Knox and I made our way out of the washroom. We were on our way back to our private room where the food hadn't stopped coming in since we'd arrived, when I felt a hand grip my shirt.

I glanced over my shoulder to see Sonya smiling at me. "Hey, Clay. It's been a while."

Sonya was a girl I'd fallen in and out of bed with many times over the past two years. She was as beautiful on the inside as she was on the outside, and I'd heard it from the guys many times how I was wasting a good thing, and I should just snap her up. We were compatible in the bedroom, that much I knew, but the rest of the stuff didn't add up.

"Sure has. How have you been?" I questioned.

She nodded, then smiled, leaning into me, "I've been good. I was just thinking about you, and I'd love it if we could spend the night together."

I nodded and looked at Knox to see he was staring off into the distance. When he looked my way and saw me answering her, he gave me a wink and turned to leave me with Sonya.

Sonya pushed her body against mine, attempting to dance with me while Knox walked away. Then she pulled her hair up into a ponytail, turned around, and rubbed her ass against me as my eyes washed over her body. She was attractive as hell, and normally I'd have my hands all over her by now, but not tonight. Something was different. I felt different, and she didn't excite me the way she had before.

"What's wrong, Clay?" she questioned when I didn't grab her. She looked up at me with those full, pouty lips.

"Sorry, sweetheart, not into it tonight, I guess," I said, placing a kiss on her cheek.

"Not tonight?" she questioned, taking offence at my answer.

"I'm sorry, Sonya, maybe next time," I said, hoping I'd let her down gently enough. I took off toward our private room.

When I walked in, the guys were all sitting around talking about the game, eating, and relaxing. I grabbed a plate and threw some food on it and then sat down over in the corner, looking for a little time for myself while I took a couple bites of the pizza they'd just delivered.

I was just about done my first slice when someone sat next to me. I turned to see Knox sitting there, looking at me while he talked on his phone. I turned my attention back to my food, but the moment he finished his call, he leaned forward and looked at me.

"I didn't expect to see you back up here," he said.

I smiled. "Why's that?"

"Sonya, that's why." He chuckled. "Figured she'd have you tied up most of the night," he said, wiggling his brows. "No pun intended, of course."

"Ah, no. We are over. She's a thing of the past now. Best left there too," I said, shoving a couple of nachos into my mouth.

"Not into her anymore?"

I studied him. Fuck, if he only knew the reason I wasn't into her anymore, but he was the last one of these guys I could ever tell. If he knew I'd had his sister in my bed last weekend, I'd be a dead man.

"I'll admit, she is a ton of fun."

"Guess that is why I'm a little shocked you're back up here." Knox chuckled.

"I should have just been honest. I'm not in the mood to be out tonight." I shrugged.

Knox nodded, looking over his shoulder at the guys. Dylan, Lucas, Levi, and Colton all sat there talking about some of their past games, laughing it up and enjoying themselves. It was nice to see the two of us opening up and welcoming the two new guys. Knox was a different story. You had to earn his trust. Normally, I'd be just like the others, but my entire being was consumed with everything else.

"Funny you should say that. I was just speaking with Lorelai and thinking of heading home. Did you want to come hang out at our place?" he questioned.

I glanced over at the other guys, knowing if I stayed here, I'd be here all night. At least if I went back to Knox's I'd be home at a decent hour.

"Let's go." I nodded.

KNOX SAT in his usual spot—the oversized chair in the corner. Lorelai was curled up on his lap, her head resting on his shoulder. It was nice to see them so happy together, I thought to myself. Reese, Knox's mom, came into the living room with a tray of coffee.

"Clay, yours is on the front left," she said, smiling as she lowered the tray in front of me.

"Thanks," I said, taking the mug carefully.

"It was so nice to see you boys on the ice tonight. I admit, I don't watch nearly enough of your games," she said, waiting as Lorelai and Knox both took their mugs.

"Well, if you didn't allow that piece of shit to dominate—"

Knox stopped speaking as Lorelai glared at him, gently shaking her head.

"Not helping," she sang, placing her fingers on his lips.

"I know, Knox. He was a mistake. I'm sorrier than anyone that I got mixed up with him," Reese said, taking a seat across from me.

"We all make mistakes," I added, looking over at Knox. "Sometimes, we have no choice but to learn the hard way."

He met my eyes, and for a moment, I felt as if I were confessing the truth about Peyton and me. That it had been a mistake, but one I'd learned something from.

"That's so true, Clay, and this unfortunately was one of my hard lessons. Now, what are you doing for the summer?" Reese questioned.

"I'm not sure. The boys are really the only family I

have, so if I'm not a part of whatever they are doing, I'm pretty much on my own."

"Oh dear, where are your parents?" she questioned. "Surely, they'd want to see you."

"Mom…" Knox said, shaking his head, basically telling her not to go there.

"It's alright, I don't mind sharing," I said, clearing my throat. "My parents and little sister unfortunately died in a house fire two months after I signed the contract to play for the Dominators."

"Oh my god," Lorelai cried out. "You never told me that!" she said, looking at Knox.

"That's because some things are to be kept private amongst us, and that is one of them," Knox answered, looking my way.

This was one thing I loved about my brothers, especially Knox, and why I was feeling so shitty about sleeping with his sister. He'd kept my horrific family secret quiet as if it were his own, just as asked, and here I was keeping something huge from him. It made me feel worse at this moment than I'd ever felt.

"Yeah, but I've never even heard about it from Phil, or on the news," Lorelai added.

"I just told you." Knox chuckled, pulling her in closer.

"No, you wouldn't of, it was something I didn't want broadcast to the entire world. So, when it happened, I paid a lot of money to have it kept quiet. The media are a bunch of sharks, but between lawyers and cash, they retreated into the woodwork as quickly as they appeared."

"Oh, Clay, I'm so sorry," Reese said, bringing her hand to her heart. "Always know you are welcome here."

"Oh, I know that. My brothers never turn me away. I just hate intruding on them, especially now that they have settled down with their women." I chuckled.

"Tell him it's fine to intrude," Lorelai said, smacking Knox in the abs. "He's welcome here at any time," she said, smacking Knox again.

"Fuck, just intrude, okay?" He chuckled, wrapping his arms around her so she couldn't hit him again, and pressed a kiss to her cheek.

"Seriously, Clay, he is serious," Reese said, giving me a gentle smile.

"I know, and I'll take him up on the offer before Lorelai bruises the crap out of him."

The four of us laughed, and soon the conversation turned to the wedding and the invitation choices. They'd narrowed the choices down while we all sat drinking our coffee. I felt my phone vibrate in my pocket and I quickly pulled it out to see who had messaged me.

I glanced at my screen and saw Peyton's name. I

swallowed hard. Reese had just mentioned she was thinking of moving to Vancouver and wondered if they'd take her to see a place close to the arena. Knox and Lorelai were both focused on the conversation.

"Excuse me for a moment," I muttered.

"Sure thing. Everything okay?" Knox asked.

"Yep, fine," I said, taking off toward the washroom. Once there, I re-read her messages.

Peyton: I don't want to bother you…

Peyton: Oh, I hope you are there…

Peyton: Shit, maybe I shouldn't have messaged you might be with my brother…

Peyton: I really need…

What the hell was going on with her? I wondered. I read her messages again and then responded.

Clay: What's wrong?

I stared at my phone, waiting to see if she was there. There was nothing, and as the seconds ticked by, it felt like forever.

"Fuck it," I muttered. I dialed her number and

waited as it rang. "Are you okay?" I whispered into the phone when I heard her answer.

She sniffled. "Not really." She cried.

"What is going on?"

I could hear her sobbing.

"I'm fucked. Knox is going to kill me," she cried. "Remember how you said I'm like family and I could come to you with anything?"

Yep, I'd said those words long before we'd slept together, but again after as well. I swallowed hard, not knowing where this conversation would go, wondering if maybe this was something her brother should be hearing.

Not wanting to go back on my word, I nodded. "Yes, what's wrong?" I asked quietly.

"I'm in trouble. When I got home, Tor came here." She sniffled.

"I think I should get your brother," I said.

I really didn't want to get in the middle of things between Knox and her, and she'd filled me in on Tor, and so had Knox after her previous visit. He was a genuine piece of work, and one I'd pray I'd never meet because my feelings toward him were the same as Knox's.

"No, Clay, don't please…he can't know I contacted you."

"Peyton, I'm really uncomfortable with this," I said, swallowing hard.

The phone went silent; I knew she was still there because I could hear her breathing along with the sobs she was trying to stifle.

"Sorry that I bothered you," she said quietly, and before I could say anything, she was gone.

I stared at my phone, waiting to see if she was going to text instead, but those three little dots never came, and just as I went to send her a message, I heard Knox call my name. I'd lost track of how long I'd been gone, so I shoved my phone in my pocket, flushed the toilet, and ran water, then opened the bathroom door to come face-to-face with Knox.

"Everything okay?" he asked.

I'd probably been gone longer than I'd thought and so I gave a fake chuckle and nodded.

"Yep, just taking a dump. I wouldn't go in there if I were you."

Chapter 8

Clay - Two Weeks Later

I SAT between Dylan and Knox, quietly reading a book as the two of them talked over me. I'd spent the better part of the last hour listening to life things, baby things, wedding things, all things, and then Dylan brought up the subject we all knew Knox rarely wanted to talk about.

"Aurora mentioned that you guys have barely heard from Peyton since she returned to Vermont."

"Yep, basically, we've heard nothing. Mom's pissed. She wanted to get on the plane tonight and come with me, but I wasn't having it. I told her I'd reach out to

Peyton and invite her to the arena for the games and find out what the hell was going on."

I swallowed hard. I'd never mentioned to Knox that I'd heard from Peyton the night I'd been at his place. I knew I should have, but I didn't want to get in the middle of their feud, even though I'd kind of put myself there. If I'd told him, he'd wonder why she'd called me, and that would also open up all kinds of questions.

"Did she respond?" Dylan questioned.

"Nope, not a fucking word. I don't even think she read the text."

"What's with her?" Dylan asked. "She wasn't always like this."

"I don't fucking know. She only continues to lie, which only makes me wonder what else she's trying to cover up. I know she messaged my mother and told her she'd paid the rent and bills with the money I'd given her, but she lied about that, too. Mom recently started getting notices from the utility companies, and then her asshole ex-boyfriend and landlord demanded she get the rent paid or he was changing the locks. I swear to god, if she spent it on drugs and shit, I'll kill her."

"Do you think it's drugs?" Dylan asked.

"I don't know what to think anymore. Mom doesn't even really know what is going on with her, I don't think."

I knew exactly what it was. She'd told me about Tor stealing money from her. In the back of my mind, I knew there was no doubt he was behind all of this, especially after the call when she'd told me he'd been there. I'd even told her she needed to be away from him, figured it may sound different coming from someone other than her brother. Besides, after seeing the guy who'd been trying to pick her up that night in a bar, these were the men she attracted. She didn't like them; I knew it, I could see it. Deep down inside, she wanted something better for herself, and I wanted to be that something for her, but I knew better. I'd already crossed a line I wasn't sure I should ever cross again.

"Maybe she is in trouble? Perhaps she is afraid to come to you?" Dylan suggested.

"She should be afraid to come to me at this point," Knox grumbled.

I slammed my book shut and looked over at him. That comment right there was the reason she refused to go to him, the reason she begged me that night not to mention anything to him, the reason she hung up on me and hadn't responded to any of my messages since. She truly was afraid to go to him.

"Why the fuck would you say something like that?" I questioned every muscle in my neck and shoulders tight.

"Clay don't get me started. You don't know the half of it," Knox grumbled.

"No, I should get you started. For someone who claims to be an amazing older brother, this proves otherwise."

"Why the fuck would you say that to me? I'm not the enemy here. Do you have any idea how much fucking money I've given her to watch her almost not only throw away her education, then to steal in front of me and my mother because it was what her boyfriend Tor taught her, the same scumbag who got her thrown out of school because he doesn't think an education is necessary. Then to watch her continue to lie to me again and again. The last time, right to my face when I asked her if she was done with him? The only reason I gave her the money this time to clear up rent and bills was because my mother wasn't going back with her. I gave her one last chance and trusted her to do the right thing, and yet, here we are again…"

"Perhaps if you would take a minute and listen to what she has to say…"

"Don't start that shit with me. I've given her chance after chance. She is literally killing my mother. It's disgusting."

"Like I said, maybe you should give her a chance to talk to you and explain…."

"Whose side are you on?" he questioned, glaring at me.

"Yours," I said, swallowing hard.

"Then why the hell are you sticking up for her when you should side with me?"

Knox glared at me like he was looking right through me. I could see the questions in his eyes, the wonder why I was making him sound like the bad guy.

"Guys, calm the hell down," Dylan said, punching me on the shoulder to pull my attention away from Knox and the situation.

"Fine," I muttered, looking toward him.

"Do you think she'll show at the arena?" Dylan asked. "Apparently, Aurora is having dinner with Lorelai and your mom tonight, and your mom has been asking," Dylan said, looking at his phone and typing a response.

I watched Knox pull his phone from his pocket and shook his head.

"Lorelai didn't message me," he said, looking over at Dylan.

Dylan chuckled. "No, because she doesn't want you to stress out, so she told Aurora to ask me to ask you. Guess it's better if I stress you out," Dylan said with a cocky smile. "You can take it out on me later on the ice."

"Or, perhaps she is just another person who doesn't

feel she can come to you when she needs something," I muttered under my breath.

Dylan lowered his phone and looked at me with an 'are you serious right now' look.

"What the fuck did you just say?" Knox said, looking at me his jaw tight.

"He said nothing," Dylan intervened, trying to keep the peace between us.

"Stay out of it, Dylan. If Clay has something to say, he should say it. Perhaps he'd like Peyton to be his problem."

I stood up, climbing over Dylan, and made my way to the back of the plane where Lucas sat with Colton and Levi and took a seat with them. Nothing good was going to come out of me saying another word to Knox, so it was best to remove myself from the situation altogether and keep my mouth shut.

THE CROWD ROARED as the buzzer went off. The puck had coasted by me, even though I'd tried to stop it, handing the game to the Ice Hawks.

"What the fuck was that, Clay?" Knox yelled as he threw his shit into his locker.

"Of course it makes logical sense to blame the goalie, but did you asses look at how you played tonight?" I yelled, throwing my jersey to the floor.

"How we played?" Colton questioned, turning to look at me. "What the fuck does that mean?"

"Yes, how you all played!"

"What the hell is that even supposed to mean?" Levi questioned. "We played like we always do, to win."

"If that was playing to win, you all better walk off this team right now."

"You are the only one who didn't give it his all tonight," Knox said, pulling his jersey off and dropping it to the floor. "Just like the last couple of games. Where the fuck has your head been?"

"Yeah, man, don't go blaming everyone else on the team," Dylan said, unlacing his skates.

"I'm not, but when we lose, we lose as a team, same with when we win, and there was not a single play on behalf of any one of you that says we were winners tonight!" I yelled.

The locker room door opened and in walked Thomkins. The entire room grew silent as he stood there staring at each one of us.

"I don't want to hear another word out of this room. Get your shit off, shower up, and get to the bus. We leave for the hotel in fifteen minutes. All the better if you'd all rather wait to shower there. Tomorrow at ten we have the ice for three hours. We are going over every play we fucked up on tonight, so we don't make this mistake tomorrow night."

The entire room was silent as he turned around and left the room, and as soon as the door closed, Knox stood up.

"You got a problem with the way we played tonight, let us have it, 'cause I sure as hell have a problem with the way you fucking played."

"Evans, I said not another fucking word, and I meant it!" Thompkins shouted from the hallway. "If I hear you speak again, I'll bench your ass tomorrow night."

"Fuck you, Thompkins," Knox muttered under his breath once the door closed, all the while glaring at me before he turned around to get changed, as did everyone else.

I kept to myself for the rest of the night. The guys headed to the restaurant for food once we got to the hotel, and even though Dylan said I should go, I declined. I wanted to be alone, so I went back to my room, took a hot shower, and watched a little TV.

There was no doubt about it. I was off my game tonight. Just like I'd been on the plane this morning listening to Knox talk about Peyton. His attitude irritated me. He was lucky to have her in his life. I'd lost my sister without warning. He did not know how that had felt, and the last thing I'd ever want for him would be to feel the pain I'd felt after losing my sister. That was why I felt it was important for him to hear her out. If she was in trouble, he should want to help her regardless of the things she'd done.

I flipped through the TV trying to find something on, and when I came up with nothing, I grabbed my sweatshirt, threw it over my head, and headed down to the bar.

IT WAS A LITTLE AFTER MIDNIGHT; the bar was empty. All the guys were probably sound asleep by now, and while we weren't supposed to drink the night before a game, but I grabbed a beer anyway and went and sat over in the corner. I needed to unwind if I was going to get any sleep tonight. I needed to clear my head and put all this behind me. Let it all go. Perhaps I needed the company of a lady tonight, and if I looked hard enough, I was certain there'd be some little puck bunny that would accompany me.

As if on command, I heard a sweet voice say my name.

Only I knew that voice all too well. Anticipation and excitement filled me, and I could feel my heart beating a little harder and faster as I glanced up to see Peyton standing there wearing a pink sweater that hugged her in all the right places and a pair of ripped jeans. She'd pulled her dirty-blonde hair back, leaving a few pieces to frame her face, and she wore a little makeup, just enough to highlight her best features.

"Nice to see you, Clay. Is it okay if I join you?"

I sat up and nodded toward the seat across from me. "Of course. Would you like anything? Beer, wine?" I questioned as the server stopped at the table, dropping off my last beer for the night.

"Ginger Ale?" she said, looking up at the server.

"Sure thing," she said as she grabbed my empty bottle.

"When did you get here?" I questioned.

"Twenty-five minutes ago," she answered, taking her jacket off.

"Talk with your brother?" I asked.

She shook her head. "No, and I'm not in the mood to talk about him, either. He told me there would be a room for me, and so I just checked in, figured I'd see him tomorrow. I'm sure he is plenty pissed off with me for not calling him or messaging him back, and after the drive, I just wanted to relax. I don't feel like any drama."

"It will be five sixty," the server said, sliding the soda in front of Peyton, waiting for payment.

"Put it on my bill," I answered, pulling my credit card from my wallet and handing it to the server as Peyton reached for her purse.

Peyton looked over at me, a tiny smile on her lips as she took a sip of the pop. "You didn't have to, but thank you," she whispered. "I've been dying for one of these, but I didn't want to pull off the highway to get one."

"So, what's been going on with you?" I questioned. "Haven't heard from you since the night you called sounding really upset."

"Sorry. I wanted to message you, but…"

"But?"

"Never mind, I realized I never should have messaged you."

"I don't play games, Peyton," I said, clearing my throat. "I told you, I'm a straight shooter, and when I said you could come to me, I meant it."

"I know, but when you mentioned I should talk to my brother, I guess I was afraid you'd go tell him and I choked."

"What happened?" I questioned.

She looked at me, worry clear in her eyes. Something had happened, and whatever it was, it hadn't been good. I was sure it had to do with the money.

"I'm sure my brother has mentioned my lack of communication, and he more than likely thinks I spent his money on alcohol or drugs."

"He mentioned something along those lines, yes."

"That figures. He already thinks he knows. He never listens to me."

"Do you blame him?" I asked.

Peyton looked up at me, her eyes lined with shock.

"Don't look at me like that. I told you; I won't sugarcoat shit."

Her eyes locked with mine.

"Do you blame him?" I repeated.

She looked around the bar, looking everywhere but at me, and when she finally met my eyes, I could see they were glassy. "No, not really."

"Why do you think that is?"

"My choices haven't been the greatest, I know that, and the lack of communication lately probably hasn't helped."

"That's a start. Peyton, I'll admit, I was shocked when you told me you weren't done with Tor."

"I am now. I see him for what he is. A cheater, a thief, a liar, an abuser, and I gave it a lot of thought. I don't want that type of relationship anymore."

"What changed your mind?"

She looked at me, sadness in her eyes. "That night

with you," she answered immediately. "I've replayed that entire night in my mind. I've never been with a man who blew my mind before. I've never been with someone I couldn't stop thinking about, and I've never been with someone who could comfort me by just thinking about the time we spent together. That was what happened."

I swallowed hard. That night hadn't left my mind since it happened. She had literally been my highlight reel for the past few weeks. I hadn't gone out. I hadn't hung out after games aside from signing autographs, and I'd turned down many nights of company with some attractive woman, all because of that night. She hadn't left my mind and was like an itch I couldn't scratch, but now that she was sitting in front of me, she was all I wanted.

"So, what happened?"

"When I returned to the house, Tor showed up at the door. At first, I thought about not letting him in, but I changed my mind. I knew I needed to end things with him. So, I let him in. He found the money Knox had given to me to take care of things, and he took it. I tried to get it back from him, but he refused. That was when I ended things with him and kicked him out. Things got a little heated."

"What do you mean, they got heated?" I questioned, feeling my muscles tighten. I swore, if he hit her, I'd drive down there tonight and put an end to him. "Did he put his…"

"No, he didn't touch me. He probably would have, but he just raised his voice and tried to take control of things, but I wouldn't let him. I stood up to him for the first time in my life."

"No, you mean you stood up for yourself, there is a difference," I said, watching her.

She nodded her head, meeting my eyes.

"You know, I think your brother would be proud of you."

"You do?"

"I do. I am. You can do so much better, Peyton. You're bright, beautiful…sexy as hell…"

"You think I'm beautiful?"

Her eyes meant mine, and I glanced away, downing the rest of the beer in the bottle. All I could think about when she looked at me was kissing those full lips agai,n and I knew if given the chance, I wouldn't be able to say no.

"Yes, I do. I think you're beautiful, and I also think it would be wise that we both say good night and go our separate ways," I said, placing the bottle down on the table.

She slipped out of the booth at the same time as I did and led the way out of the bar to the elevator.

Once inside, I pressed the button to the 12th floor and glanced at her.

"Thirteen," she said.

The doors closed, and we both stood there looking forward. It was almost as if we were afraid to look at one another. I could feel the tension building in the small elevator as I looked up to see we'd only moved about three floors. I shifted my stance when I felt her hand slip into mine.

I looked over at her—first at her lips, then at her eyes. Want and desire screamed inside of me. Each second that passed I could feel myself growing weaker until, in one quick motion, I pulled her into my arms, kissing her hard.

The moment her lips touched mine, the ache that had been running through me quieted and everything that had been building inside of me felt at peace. When the elevator stopped at my floor, I didn't think twice. I pulled her with me, leading her to my room.

Chapter 9

Peyton

OVER THE PAST couple of days, I'd not only got to spend a couple nights with Clay, but I finally explained everything that had happened to my brother. For the first time that I could remember, Knox sat and listened to everything I had to tell him without saying a word, and when I say everything, I held nothing back regarding the situation with Tor. I wanted him to trust me; I needed him to trust me, because I didn't want bad blood between us any longer.

"I'm proud of you, Peyton," Knox said, shoveling food into his mouth at lunch.

"Thanks."

"Seriously, it took a lot for you to do that, and I'm glad you did it."

"It did, but, Knox, it felt so good to get rid of him."

"It's only going to go up from here," he said, nodding at the dessert menu. "Pick something, whatever you want."

I opened the menu and immediately decided on the apple crumble. It wasn't something I ever ate—hated it actually—but one look at the picture and I could almost smell and taste the apples and cinnamon.

"What are you going to have?" he asked.

"Apple crumble."

Knox gave me a questioning glance. "Peyton, you hate apple crumble."

It was true; I hated apple crumble. It was something that my mother had made on a weekly basis when I grew up, and yet I'd only ever tried it one time, immediately hating it. However, looking at the picture on the menu, it looked so good it caused my stomach to grumble.

"It's like it's calling to me." I giggled.

"Okay, well, we will make it two, and if you don't want yours after all, I'll just eat it." Knox chuckled. "Then you can choose something you'll actually like."

The two of us grew quiet while Knox checked his phone. Then I cleared my throat.

"Knox, I've given moving some thought as well," I said, closing the menu.

"And?" he asked, placing his phone on the table.

"And if Mom moves to Vancouver, then I'm on board. I think the change of city, of pace, might do me good."

"Great, I'll have to let Mom know. She'll be so excited to hear this."

"No, please don't tell her. I'd like to be the one to let her know."

Knox nodded. "Sure thing. I promise I won't say a word."

When the server approached, Knox ordered our desert and then turned his attention back to me. "Oh, by the way, where were you last night?" he questioned.

"What do you mean? I was in my room," I said, swallowing hard.

Knox shook his head. "No, I stopped by, knocked, and waited. There was no answer."

"What time? I could have been in the shower," I answered.

"A little after eleven thirty."

I could feel my cheeks heating. A little after eleven, I'd wandered down to Clay's room using the stairs to avoid the possibility of being caught by Knox or any other guy on the team. I'd seen Colton slip into his room at the far end of the hall and was certain he'd caught sight of me just as Clay had opened the door.

I shifted in my seat. "You're sure you had the right room?"

"Pretty sure. I did book it."

"Why are you asking?" I questioned, folding the corner of my napkin, hoping I didn't sound suspicious.

"Colton mentioned he thought he saw you outside of Clay's door a little before eleven. Guess I'm paranoid. I'm in the room beside him, and I know he had some company last night. I could hear them through the wall. I was going to knock on his door after Colton messaged me, but figured I'd check on you instead of bothering Clay."

"Oh wait, I ran down to the store in the lobby to grab a snack before they closed. While I was there, I got a message from Elsie letting me know she was coming over for dinner when I get back. Then she called me."

"What snack did you get?" he questioned.

Immediately, I answered the first thing I thought of. "Skittles."

I hated skittles more than I hated apple crumble. I did not know why I'd picked the only piece of candy I hated.

I knew why, because I panicked. I'd had no choice

but to lie to him about this, otherwise the pair of us would be disowned.

"You hate skittles."

"Oh, not anymore. They are my new favourite. Elsie got me hooked on them, and I can't get enough of them."

Just then, the server returned with our apple crumble and slid the two pieces in front of each of us. Knox picked up his fork, digging into his, while I did the same.

"Well, I hope you enjoyed them, and I hope you enjoy this desert," Knox said, watching as I took my first bite.

I was so glad my brother was proud of me for standing up for myself, which only made the fact I'd just lied to him make me feel even worse. We ate our dessert and then made our way over to the arena where I watched as they beat the Ice Hawks five to nothing in the last game here in Vermont.

I waited around, hoping to not only say goodbye to my brother but to sneak off with Clay for a few minutes before they left, but immediately they were swept off to the airport shortly after they'd got out of the locker room.

I made my way back to the hotel and spent one more night alone, and in the morning, I drove back home, making it in time for my shift at work.

"SO, are you really thinking of moving to Vancouver?" Elsie asked as she cubed up the chicken she'd brought for dinner.

I was so excited to have something home cooked that I was practically salivating. The last couple of days I'd eaten dinner with the team, and even Knox mentioned how my appetite had picked up. I'd been hungrier than normal, but then I'd barely eaten for weeks after Tor and William had been at the house. I hadn't mentioned that to him, though, mainly because I didn't want him to worry about me.

"I think so. Honestly, it makes the most sense. Tor and I are over. My boss is being an enormous dick, and well, don't forget the nightmare that is William."

"How could I forget that? I can't believe your mom entered a relationship with that guy. He's so icky."

I giggled. "I know, but then you say that about me and Tor."

"Honestly, Tor is icky too, but it's not just that. It's because I know what kind of jackass he is." She giggled. "Pass me the potatoes."

I grabbed the small bag of potatoes she'd brought

to her and watched as she cut those up as well. "What are we having again?"

"Curry chicken and potato in roti. You are going to love it," she said, winking at me.

"Hope you are right," I said, never having tried that dish before.

She added the potatoes to the boiling pot of water and then added the chicken into a pan, letting it cook.

"How was your stay in Vancouver?"

I'd not mentioned anything that had happened in Vancouver this time to anyone. Elsie was my best friend, and I still wasn't even comfortable enough to mention my time with Clay. I'd told her about my previous stay and running into him the night Knox had made me face security for stealing. I'd told her about the drinks we'd shared and how we'd spent some time getting to know one another. I'd told her about the kiss we'd shared that night in the car and how he'd profusely apologized afterward when he dropped me off. I'd told her how we'd shared the occasional text message after that, how he'd check in on me, but that ended about a month later, and since then I'd not mentioned his name.

"It was good."

"What about Vermont? I saw they kicked the Ice Hawks' ass."

"Yeah, it was a good time, and I finally patched

things up with my brother. He was happy to hear things are over between Tor and I."

"Good, I still can't believe that you and Tor are over. What brought that on?"

The memory of Clay invaded my mind. His words that night in the bar in Vancouver, and everything that had happened afterward, had been the start. If it hadn't happened before, it would have happened after this past weekend. I could still feel the way he'd gently caressed my cheek and ran his fingers through my hair while gently kissing me. The way his eyes had skimmed my naked body, right down to his touch and the way he'd slowly fucked me until I came. Never one time had he come before I did, and he never cared how long it took either. Not that it ever took long with him.

"I don't know, just tired of his games, I guess."

Elsie looked over at me. "No, no way, there's something else?" she said, pointing the knife she had in her hand in my direction.

I shrugged. I could feel my cheeks heat and gave her a small smile.

"You met someone?" she said, her eyes growing wide with excitement.

I shook my head, looking away.

"Peyton, don't hold out on me!" She laughed as she bent over and looked at me.

"I'm not, there isn't…there isn't anyone to talk about," I said, hoping she'd drop the topic.

"Come on, just tell me about him. I know there is someone. I can see it in your eyes."

Taking a deep breath, I looked over at her and slowly nodded. "Okay, fine, I met someone, and while there isn't anything other than a few amazing nights together, I realized maybe I don't need to be treated like trash, that maybe there really are good guys out there."

"There are good guys out there. Sometimes, you just need to weed through the shit to get to them. Do you think if you were to move to Vancouver, you might see this mystery man again? I mean, I'm only guessing that is where he is."

I nodded. "Well, I shouldn't say a definite yes, but I know I'd want to see him again. Not sure what he wants, though."

"Are you going to give me any other details about him?"

I shook my head; not sure I wanted to divulge it was one of Knox's teammates. I was still feeling odd about the whole situation in that regard. Especially after Knox admitted to me that he heard us the other night. Not that he knew it was us, but it still made me uncomfortable. Plus, I knew Knox was overprotective of me. He always had been after my father had left.

He'd often tell me he didn't want to see me grow up without a father like he had, so in his own way, he'd stepped into the role.

"Fine, make me wait to find out about the guy who pulled you away from Tor. Something the rest of us have been trying to do for many months. It was becoming exhausting to be honest, so I'm glad it happened." Elsie giggled, letting out a sigh. "He must be something. While we wait, why don't you pass me that bag of spice there?" she said, pointing to a small clear bag containing yellow powder.

"What's that?"

"The magic spice—the curry," she said, winking as she drained the potatoes and quickly mashed them, then added a couple of teaspoons of spice to the potato mixture and then to the chicken that was simmering.

"Take a smell of this," she said, moving out of the way for me to come in.

The moment I leaned over the pot a rush of saliva filled my mouth, and my stomach turned. I tried to swallow but couldn't and bolted toward the bathroom off the kitchen, slamming the door shut behind me, making it to my knees in front of the toilet just in time for me to be sick.

I heard Elsie knock on the door, but between being

sick and trying to catch my breath, I couldn't answer her.

"Peyton, Peyton, are you okay?" she cried, cracking the door open a bit.

I looked over at her and shook my head. She stepped into the washroom, came over and gathered my hair, holding it back in time for the next wave of nausea to hit.

I'D GOTTEN a bit of clear broth down, but the smell of curry that still lingered throughout the house was still making me feel sick.

"Are you sure you're okay?" Elsie asked.

She'd profusely apologized, but I assured her it wasn't her cooking that had made me sick, since I'd not even tasted it.

"I'll be okay. I don't know where that even came from," I said, relaxing in the chair in the living room with a cool cloth across the back of my neck.

"While you rest, did you want to watch an episode of *Friends*?" Elsie questioned.

I rested my head against the back of the chair and

nodded. We'd been watching the show since my mother had recommended it, and so far, we were loving it. As we sat there watching the next episode, I looked at my phone, noticing the date. It had been almost four weeks since I'd returned from Vancouver. My stomach slightly flipped again, causing another rush of saliva to my mouth as I quickly thought about that trip and then realized I should have gotten my period two weeks ago. With everything that had gone on, I hadn't realized I'd missed it.

I shifted in my chair, pulling my legs up underneath as Elsie let out a laugh at something Chandler had said.

"Why aren't you laughing?" she questioned, pausing the show.

"What?" I questioned, looking up from my phone.

"Peyton, what is it? You look like you've seen a ghost," Elsie said.

"Sorry what?" I asked again, closing the calendar on my phone.

The possibility of pregnancy swirled around in my mind as I looked at Elsie. The possibility of who the father might be was making me feel sick again.

"Are you okay?" she asked again, this time turning her full attention to me. "You look like you are going to be sick again."

"Can you drive me to the pharmacy?" I questioned, looking at her, trying hard to stop the burning in my eyes from the tears that were threatening to fall.

"Why? Need some anti-nausea medication?" she questioned. "I might have some in my purse, actually," she said, getting up off the couch and heading toward the entryway.

"No, not anti-nausea medication. However, if you have a pregnancy test in that bottomless purse of yours, I'll gladly take that instead."

FOUR DAYS LATER, Elsie and I sat on the edge of my bed staring down at those stupid little pink lines once again. My heart was racing, and it was making me feel lightheaded.

"Well, no doubt about it, you are pregnant. I don't think we need to do any more of these," she said, pulling the last test from my hand.

"Maybe one more, just for good measure."

"Good measure? Why? Do you think test number six is faulty too?" She giggled, throwing it into the garbage.

"Oh, I don't know, hoped is more like it," I said, running my fingers through my hair.

I'd been in touch with my mother, who had told me Knox would pick me up at the airport tonight. My mind had been on so many other things, I still hadn't packed, and I knew I needed to if I was going to make my flight.

"Maybe, to ease your mind, you should just make an appointment with your doctor," Elsie said, sitting down beside me.

"Or we could do one more drugstore run," I said, picking at the side of my fingernail.

Elsie picked up my phone and handed it to me. "Seriously, just call. After six tests, I can guarantee what the next one is going to tell you."

"I can't book an appointment. I'm leaving for Vancouver tonight. Did you forget?" I sighed.

"I didn't forget. Book it for when you get back. Do you know who the father is?" she questioned. "If it's the mystery man, perhaps you can meet up and talk with him. Might ease a little of this anxiety you're feeling if you share this with him."

"Perhaps," I whispered, knowing that if it were Tor's instead of Clay's, it would only increase my anxiety. I took the phone and dialed the doctor's office. "I'll book, and then will you help me pack?" I asked.

"Of course," she said, getting up off the bed and pulling out my suitcase from the closet.

Once I hung up the phone, I walked over to my

closet and pulled out a few clothes, passing them to Elsie.

"Are you going to shed some light?" she questioned.

I nodded, swallowing hard.

"Is it Tor's?" she asked, folding my sweaters carefully and placing them in my bag.

I let out the breath I was holding. For so many reasons, I didn't want to disclose things, but I needed someone to talk to.

"I don't think so. It's been almost eight weeks since we were last together, and we used protection."

"So then, the baby's father is the guy from Vancouver?"

Instantly, my mind went to Clay. To that first night, and the other nights in Vermont. I'd heard Knox talk about him, about what kind of player he was, and while I knew he'd been with many women, I didn't think he was as bad as Knox and the other guys made him out to be. In fact, I didn't find him to be a player at all.

"I think so," I whispered.

"Do you…do you know how to get in touch with him?" she asked.

I nodded, sniffling at the same time. The fear of having to admit things to my family, to my brother, scared me to death. I wasn't sure how he'd take it.

Actually, that wasn't true. I knew how Knox would take it, and it wouldn't be well. In fact, I'd probably end up raising the baby alone after Knox finished him.

"Maybe you should call him. There is probably a good chance that Tor isn't the father, after all. Maybe you should just let him know that something is up, but that—"

"But what?" I said, whipping around.

Elsie looked at me, a guilty look on her face.

"That what?" I asked again. "Let me guess, that I'll take care of it?" I said, swallowing hard.

Elsie slowly nodded her head. "I…well…I figured you'd want to put the baby up for adoption or something. I mean, in a couple of months, you'll graduate and be ready to start up your career."

"Elsie, I don't know what I'm going to do. I don't even know how Clay is even going to feel about this. He's on the road so much, and I doubt he wants to be tied down with me and a baby," I whispered.

"Clay? As in Clay Harris?" Elsie questioned as she placed the pants she'd folded into the suitcase. "You got involved with Clay Harris?"

I looked over my shoulder at her, not realizing I'd said his name out loud, or that she'd be able to guess right away who the other party was to the mess I was in. When I said nothing right away, I'd practically admitted to her she was correct.

"You slept with your brother's teammate?" she questioned again.

I slowly nodded my head as shock lined her face.

"What about the promise you made to your brother?"

I swallowed hard. Yep, the promise I'd made that I still now felt like shit about. Secretly, I'd always had a thing for Clay, and he'd only been doing what Knox would have expected—protecting me from being picked up by someone who would have probably become more of an issue than Tor. Neither of us had planned for things to go as far as they did. At least, not the first time.

"It's not like we planned for this to happen, it just sort of did," I said, anxiety creeping into my body, a tear slipping down my cheek.

"Oh, Peyton," she whispered, coming up behind me and wrapping her arms around me. "What are you going to do?"

I stared ahead and placed my hands on her arms, thinking for a moment. "I guess I am just going to take it one day at a time. Wait until I see my doctor and go from there. Now, can we finish packing so that I don't miss my flight?"

"Sure thing, and call your doctor's office back and give them my number. That way, you can keep things somewhat quiet and deal with it when you get back."

Chapter 10

Peyton

KNOX AND MOM picked me up from the airport, and the three of us went for dinner. Now we were back at the house, and I lay in the spare room watching TV. Lorelai was in bed, Mom was watching TV in the living room, and Knox had gone out with the guys.

The moment I got into the car, Mom immediately asked me if I was planning to move to Vancouver, and while I wanted to tell her yes, I hadn't. Things had changed since I found out the news of the pregnancy. If this were Tor's baby, which it very well could be, but probably wasn't, then he had the right to be in his child's life. If it was Clay's baby, well, he had a right as well, but until I found out just how far along I was, I'd have to wait to give her an answer. It was the only conclusion I'd come to on the flight here.

The worst part of the entire situation had been the searing look I'd gotten from Knox as he stared at me through the rearview mirror when I'd told my mother, followed by the look of disappointment at my answer.

I couldn't get the look out of my mind as I rolled over onto my side and picked up my phone, messaging Elsie. I'd done as she suggested and left my doctor's office with her number instead of my cell phone. I didn't want to be questioned about anything right now. I was scared, confused, and felt so alone in all this. I wanted to tell my mother and my brother, but I knew he'd jump to conclusions and finish it with 'I told you so.' That wasn't exactly the support system I needed right now.

I quickly messaged Elsie, then placed my phone back on the table, turning my attention back to the movie I was watching. The moment my phone vibrated; I grabbed it.

Elsie: Appointment booked for next week.

PEYTON: Okay.

Elsie: Did you talk to Clay?

PEYTON: No, not yet. He doesn't even know I'm in town. Plus, I didn't think going out tonight would be wise. I really don't want to rock the boat right now with my brother. He's already angry with me again.

Elsie: Why? What happened?

PEYTON: Mom asked me when I was planning on moving out here when they all picked me up at the airport. I was honest and told her I didn't know yet.

Elsie: Why would you say that? I thought you made up your mind.

PEYTON: I was being honest. That was what Knox wanted.

ELSIE: Yes, but I don't understand, you wanted to move.

PEYTON: I do, but...

ELSIE: Then I don't get it. What's the bloody issue?

PEYTON: What if the baby is Tor's don't you think he had the right...

Elsie: Peyton, stop. We both know
that it's not Tor's. We also both know,
or at least I know, that even if it was,
he'd want no part of it. I think you
know that as well, but because you
are afraid it might be his, you're afraid
of admitting the truth to yourself.

PEYTON: What truth would that be?

ELSIE: That if it were Tor's he'd not
want any part of it, and even if he said
he did you'd definitely not want him to
be a part of it.

I stared at her words. God she was so right. There'd be no way I'd want him involved, even if he wanted to be. I already knew that. I closed my eyes and rested my head on my pillow. My head was pounding.

PEYTON: Can I message you in a bit?

ELSIE: Of course you can. I'll be up. I
need to finish this paper I'm working on.

PEYTON: Oh, what time is my
appointment

ELSIE: Two in the afternoon on
Wednesday.

PEYTON: Thanks, talk to you soon.

I shut my phone off. I didn't want to be bothered. I needed to spend time alone, figure things out. I shut the TV off, rolled over and faced the wall, closing my eyes. Things would work out. They had to.

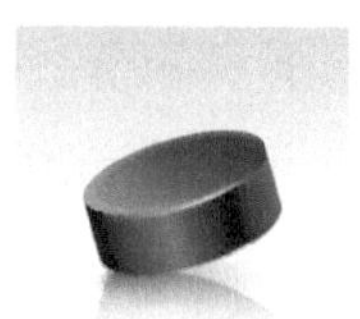

"PEYTON, how about you crumble the cheese for the lasagna?" Mom said, passing me the containers of ricotta cheese and a bowl.

I swallowed hard as I looked down at the cheese in the container, feeling my stomach turn. I'd been sick most of today. Thankfully, Knox had left early for practice, and Mom and Lorelai had gone grocery shopping, so each time I'd been sick, I'd been alone. It happened first thing in the morning while I'd been in the shower and then again late morning just before they'd returned.

"If you'd prefer to deal with the noodles, I can do the cheese." Lorelai said, a look of concern on her face as she looked at me.

"Thanks. I never liked the feel of this cheese," I said, glancing at my mother, who gave me a curious look.

I switched spots with Lorelai and stirred the pot of noodles.

"They should be almost done," Mom said. "We don't want to overcook them as they will continue to cook in the oven.

"I know. Who's all coming for dinner?" I asked, stirring the pot again before placing the strainer Lorelai had given me in the sink. "Looks like there is going to be enough food to feed and army."

"Well, we asked Lucas and Ella, Dylan and Aurora, of course, and the two new players on the team, Levi and Colton. But so far, we've only heard from Dylan and Aurora. It's okay though, because even if no one else shows up, Dylan and Knox eat about as much as the four of us do." Lorelai giggled.

"That they do," Mom said. "Your grocery bill must be huge."

"It is."

"Oh, did you hear if Clay was coming? He seems like such a nice young man," Mom asked.

My head perked up when I heard Clay's name. I wasn't expecting to see him this visit.

"No, Clay hasn't accepted either," Lorelai answered. "Although, I don't know if Knox even asked him when I told him to. He was supposed to invite him when I first brought it up, which was when they were out in Vermont, but the man apparently had other things on his mind. Something about winning some hockey game." Lorelai giggled.

"That sounds like my son."

"I don't know how you dealt with him, Reese. I really don't." Lorelai giggled.

"Has he asked him yet?" I questioned, swallowing hard. I could hear the anticipation in my voice.

"He's apparently doing so today. We shall see," Lorelai said, still crumbling the cheese and not paying any attention to the sound of my voice, thankfully.

I glanced over to see my mother staring at me. Her face held another questioning look, but all she did was give me a small smile.

"Peyton, honey, those noodles are probably done," she said.

I shut the stove off and drained the pot of noodles into the strainer, then placed the strainer inside the pot and filled it with cold water to stop the noodles from cooking, just like my mother had taught me.

"So, I know Dylan and Aurora, but Lucas and Ella?" I questioned.

"Yeah, Lucas Clark and Ella Larson, although now it's Clark. Ella works in the PR department, but they aren't coming. They already had plans to have dinner with her father. He owns the Dominators," Lorelai said.

"Oh, he's dating the owner's daughter?"

"More like married the owner's daughter. In Vegas, she thought the entire thing was fake. It was crazy."

"Fake?" I questioned.

"Yep, she thought those little chapels all over Vegas were all fake. I guess she'd read somewhere that some of them were fake and figured they all were, so when his mother put forth the idea of marriage, she accepted."

"Oh wow, I'd love to hear their entire story. Too bad they won't be here."

"Don't you worry. When you move here, you'll be on the inside. I'll drag you to every game and we'll have girls' nights when the guys are on the road. You're going to love it. Maybe we can even find you an eligible bachelor on the team," Lorelai said, shoving the bowl of ricotta into the centre of the large kitchen island.

"Clay would be a good option; don't you think Lorelai? Do you know if he is involved with anyone?"

"Don't believe so, at least I never hear him speak of anyone."

I could feel my face heat at her suggestion. I looked over at my mother and noticed she was watching me, a curious look on her face. I had to do something besides just stand here with flushed cheeks, so I let out a laugh and held up my hands.

"No, no hockey guys for me. I lived with my brother, remember? I know what sort of trouble they can be. Plus, I've had my fair share of trouble with the guys I have dated, so I think, to be fair to myself and give myself a chance to heal, I might just stay single for a while," I said.

"You say that now but just wait. Wait until one of them sinks their teeth into you. They are persistent when they set their eyes on something. Just as persistent as they are about the game. Trust me."

"Did Aurora feel that way, too?" I asked.

"Oh goodness, yes. Her situation was different, though, but Dylan wouldn't give up either once he found her again. Another thing about these men, they can also be hard to say no to."

"Reminds me of Knox's father. He was like that as well, persistent and impossible to turn away," Mom said.

"That must be where he gets it from." Lorelai giggled.

"Be thankful that is the only quality he got from that man," Mom said, building the layers of the lasagna.

"So, Peyton, when are you thinking of moving out here?" Lorelai questioned.

I glanced over at my mother. Lorelai hadn't been with Knox and Mom when they'd picked me up last night, and while I didn't know her all that well, I knew she always made me feel welcome when I was here.

"I'm thinking maybe a month from now," I answered.

The moment the words fell from my mouth, my mother turned and looked at me. I could see she was wondering why I hadn't answered her that way last night, but until I'd talked to Elsie and she'd made me realize that, even if Tor was the father of my baby, I wouldn't want him in my life, I knew moving was the option to choose.

"Well, we can't wait to have you closer. Same with you, Reese. I am so happy that you're both moving out here."

"Well, hopefully we are. If we can find a place to live, that is. That last place was gorgeous, but man, it was costly."

"It was, but like Knox said, he has no problem paying the rent for the year until you are situated here and have a job. Especially if you liked the place. Plus, the doctors here pay way better too for any office administrators than they do out there as well. If you get into a specialist's office, which I can't see you having a problem with what with your experience, then you'll be set."

"We'll have to see. I want Peyton to like the place as well. I'm sure she'll want a say."

I nodded and passed Mom the noodles, just as my stomach spun.

"Peyton? Are you feeling okay?" Mom questioned.

"Yes, why?" I asked.

"Honey, you're pale." She said coming over and placing her hand on my forehead. "Clammy to the touch as well. I think you should go lie down for a bit."

My stomach spun again, and this time a rush of saliva filled my mouth. Swallowing hard I nodded, "I think I'm just going to go lay down for a bit," I said, looking at both Mom and Lorelai.

Neither of them said anything as I left the room. I felt hot but cool at the same time. I'd just shut the door to my room and sat down on my bed when the door opened, and my mother walked in.

"Peyton, are you alright?" Mom asked sitting down next to me. She yelled at Lorelai to bring a glass of water.

"I'm fine. Just tired," I answered. "I didn't sleep all that well last night."

I felt my stomach turn, and before I could shove Mom out of the way and run to the bathroom, I grabbed the garbage pail in my room and emptied the contents of my stomach.

Lorelai appeared in the doorway with a glass of water, just as I threw up again.

"Lorelai, honey, can you grab a cool cloth," Mom asked, holding my hair back.

When I felt the cloth on the back of my neck and my stomach stopped spinning, I looked up at my mother. She cleared her throat as she placed the cloth on my face, wiping away the sweat from my forehead.

"How far along are you?" she questioned, giving me a knowing look.

I could feel my cheeks heat as she stared at me. Then I looked over at Lorelai to see her standing there, watching everything unfold.

"I don't know. I'll find out when I see the doctor next week," I replied knowing there was no point in trying to hide this.

"Do you know who the father is?" Mom questioned.

I slowly nodded but didn't respond.

"You don't have to tell me, but I hope you will confide in me when you're ready. I want you to know that this won't go any further than the confines of this room, right, Lorelai."

"You got it. Secrets are safe with the two of us," she added.

Mom handed me the cool cloth and got up off the bed. She walked to the door, pulling it closed, and the two of them left me to rest. I was sure that I wasn't fooling either of them. They weren't dumb, they'd be able to put two and two together. My questions about Clay, the sound of my voice, surely would have given the answer away as to who the father was. I just prayed they'd keep the secret away from my brother.

Chapter 11

Clay

I GLANCED down at my phone and saw I had an unread text message from Peyton. A smile came to my lips as I glanced around the room, making sure that Knox wasn't behind me, before I opened her message.

> PEYTON: When you get a minute, I'd like to talk to you. Can you please message me?

I frowned. We'd been messaging on and off since we'd gotten back from Vermont, and she had never started a message this way. Normally, they were fun and playful, some were flirty, and occasionally her messages were sexy as hell. Our phone conversations had been the same, but this, this was different. It was direct and to the point.

I quickly typed back, asking if everything was okay, and waited for a few seconds to see if she responded. When I heard Knox's voice and then his laugh coming toward me, I quickly shoved my phone into my locker. He came walking in with Levi and made his way over to his locker, before turning to me.

"Hey, man, Lorelai wants to know if you are planning on joining us for dinner tonight?" Knox questioned as he pulled his jeans and sweater from his locker. "Her and Mom are making a huge Italian meal —lasagna, garlic bread, meatballs and some sinful desert that will probably add ten pounds to us. We probably shouldn't eat it before the game, but what the hell?"

"Is that an invitation or is that Lorelai telling me I should be there?" I chuckled.

Ever since Lorelai found out that something had happened to my family, she'd been trying to include me anywhere and everywhere she could, which I appreciated, but I didn't want it to become a habit because I didn't want her to feel that she had to.

Knox laughed. "Let's just say you better be there. I forgot to ask when we were in Vermont, so I've sort of been in the doghouse, until last night that is," he said, raising his eyebrows in gest.

We'd just finished practice and had tonight off, along with most of tomorrow, when we played the sixth game of the seven with the Ice Hawks.

"Anyone else from the team coming?" I asked, dropping my towel and slipping into my grey Dominator joggers and sweatshirt.

"Dylan and Aurora will be there. I've put the invite to Lucas and Ella, and Levi and Colton, as she would like to meet them, but the only ones we've heard from are Ella and Lucas, until today that is. They unfortunately cannot make it. Poor guy is having dinner with her dad. Levi here said he has some sort of date to go on, and Colton still hasn't answered yet."

"Shit, glad I'm not Lucas." I chuckled.

The last person I'd want to have dinner with was Larson. Yet he took the news of them marrying way better than we all thought he would. We'd been prepared to give Lucas a sendoff, but thankfully, it didn't come to that. Although, if Knox ever found out that his sister and I had been together, maybe I'd wish I were having dinner with Larson and fucking his daughter instead. He seemed less scary than Knox; and I knew when Knox found out, because let's face it, it was only a matter of time, I probably wouldn't be playing hockey any longer, because Knox would make sure I couldn't.

"Yeah, sure, I'll be there. Don't want you in the doghouse with Lorelai." I chuckled.

"I don't want to be in the doghouse, either. It's a hell of a place to be."

"I'm sure. I've got to get going. See you at what, seven?"

"Be there for six. We'll have drinks and talk game talk while the girls help my mom getting everything out on the table."

"Sounds good."

I SPLASHED a bit of cologne on my neck, grabbed the two bottles of wine I'd picked up earlier for tonight, and headed out the door. I still hadn't heard a response from Peyton and wondered if I should call her on my way for dinner but decided against it. She was probably at work and wouldn't be able to talk. It was the only reason I could think why she hadn't messaged me back, and since I'd have limited time to talk, I made a mental note to call her later tonight once I was home, when we could have some privacy.

"Clay, I'm so glad to see you," Lorelai greeted as she opened the door and stepped to the side, letting me in.

She smiled as I handed her the two bottles of wine I'd brought. "Thank you, these are lovely," she said, leaning in and placing a kiss on my cheek. "You really didn't have to go to the trouble."

"I wanted to." I winked, pulling her against me for a hug and another quick peck on the cheek.

"Hey, hey…no man better be kissing my wife." Knox chuckled as he came over, greeting me with a fist bump, handing me a bottle of water.

"Slow down there, she's still fair game. She isn't your wife yet." I chuckled.

"Watch him!" Dylan shouted from inside the house. "He loves kissing Aurora, too."

"Are you really that insecure?" Aurora yelled back as she poked her head around the corner from where she was in the kitchen. She waved and then smiled my way.

"Yeah, what she said. Besides, what's the problem, jealous?" Lorelai questioned, looking at Knox before leaning in and kissing my cheek again. "Afraid I may run off with Clay and that he'll satisfy me better than you do," she said, patting my chest.

"Hey, don't you dare bring me into your little love den. You will run away with me if you do," I said, pulling her against me as she giggled. "Don't deny it, you know it's true."

Knox shook his head. "Kill it, Harris." He chucked, looking at Lorelai.

"Yes, please, kill it!" Dylan shouted again, causing us all to laugh.

"Just stating facts," I said.

"Remember that thing I did last night?" Knox questioned, his voice low enough, even I could barely hear him as he looked her straight in the eye.

I looked at Lorelai and saw her cheeks flush as she looked at me.

"Yes."

"Would you like it again? If you do, you won't go kissing another man." He pulled her to his side and chuckled as he hugged her tight.

"Insecure much…" I chuckled as I looked at Knox.

"Shut up! I'm not insecure. Just reminding her what she has."

"Why do you feel the need, she never had me to begin with, so it's not necessary."

"Guys, that's enough. This is a stupid conversation." Lorelai giggled as she looked at me and smiled as she shook her head. "I'm not running off with anyone, and thanks for the wine, Clay."

"You're welcome." I winked, following Knox into

the living room to find Dylan watching the sports channel.

"Hey, man," I said, grabbing a seat on the couch across from Dylan, who was chugging back a bottle of water.

"'Bout time you got here. We need to talk strategy for the game tomorrow," he said, leaning forward. "Rest of the guys should be here, too. After all, we are the starting lineup."

"Ah, we'll plan, then fill them in," I said.

I glanced into the kitchen to see a very pregnant Aurora sitting on a kitchen stool making a salad, while Lorelai and Reese were busy rolling meatballs. I was just about to turn my attention to what the guys were saying when I saw movement in the hallway.

Peyton came around the corner wearing a dark pair of jeans and a beige sweater. My eyes ran over her curves as she glanced in my direction. She gave me a tiny but awkward smile and then went to stand beside her mother. I had no clue she was going to be here, but I was glad she was. Like before, she'd not been far from my mind, and I hoped that we'd have a chance to talk at some point tonight.

The three of us got down to business and began planning our strategy for the upcoming games, and then, when asked, Dylan and Knox got up to help the girls out in the kitchen. I'd noticed Peyton had excused herself from the kitchen a while ago, and I was curious about where she'd gone, so I quietly took off down the hall toward the bathroom.

I was just about to open the door when the door pulled open, and Peyton stood before me. Her eyes were bloodshot, almost like she'd been crying.

"Everything okay?" I asked quietly, not wanting anyone to hear me. She looked a little pale.

She looked over my shoulder down the hall and then pulled me into the bathroom and closed the door, locking it.

Standing there, ringing her hands together, she looked to the floor instead of at me. Something was wrong, I could tell. I'd never seen her like this before. Even the night that I'd run into her in the bar after she'd dealt with security and the police for shoplifting, she wasn't this worked up.

"Where is my brother?" she asked, quietly.

"Everyone's in the kitchen putting the finishing touches on dinner. It's almost ready."

"Shouldn't you be out there helping?" she questioned.

"Don't worry about me."

She nodded and then turned away from me and began pacing back and forth. "I messaged you."

"I know. I responded, but you didn't answer me back."

"I know. I don't know why I didn't respond," she mumbled, still not facing me.

"When did you get here? Why didn't you tell me you were coming?"

"Knox picked me up last night," she whispered, finally turning to look at me.

"Are you feeling okay?" I questioned, taking in her pale skin tone and flushed cheeks. I placed my hand on her cheek. Her skin was cool to the touch; despite looking like she was on fire.

She bit her bottom lip and brought her eyes to mine and shook her head.

"What is it?" I asked.

"I um, I found out...I'm pregnant," she whispered.

As I stood there, Peyton watching me, I went from being fine one moment to my mind whizzing as her words registered in my mind. She was pregnant. She was pregnant. The words repeated over and over as I stared at her.

I was certain the color had drained from my face as well. Then as I stood there looking at her, while she waited for a response, I mentally did the math from the first time we were together until now. It had been almost six weeks, and from what I remembered, that was about the time Aurora had showed signs of morning sickness.

Was it mine?

We'd used a condom. I'd checked to make sure the sucker hadn't ripped, which it hadn't. As I stood there staring back at her, it came to me. The last time we'd done it that first night, I'd run out of them. Desperate for more of her, I'd slipped inside of her without a condom. I'd planned on pulling out…

I guess it didn't matter now, I thought to myself. The one and only time I'd ever gone unprotected… My eyes landed on Peyton's, and I was about to ask her what I should have immediately questioned, instead of trying to conclude myself, but she'd already walked over to the door and opened it, stepping out into the hall. She didn't even look back at me. She walked out and shut the door, leaving me in the bathroom.

Chapter 12

Peyton

CLAY HAD BEEN quiet all during dinner. He'd barely said two words, even when the conversation had turned toward the game, despite my brother and Dylan trying to pull him into the conversation. He wouldn't even look at me once we moved into the living room, where we all enjoyed the dessert Lorelai had made. I'd even attempted to speak with him when he helped me bring the dessert dishes into the kitchen. It hadn't helped that Mom came buzzing in and started making coffee for everyone. Shortly after, he quietly slipped from the house.

Once everyone was gone and we'd all turned in for

the night, I lay in my room, my mind spinning. Even though I'd thought I wanted Clay to know, perhaps it had been a mistake to tell him tonight. Maybe it was the wrong time. Maybe I should have waited until I was certain that the baby was his. Or maybe I shouldn't have said anything at all. That might have been better, I thought to myself.

I shoved my phone on the charger and pulled the blankets up over me, trying to get comfortable. I rolled over, hugging the pillow close to me, when my phone vibrated. I'd already spoken to Elsie, and it was late. I ignored it instead, but it started vibrating again a few minutes later, and then once more.

Maybe it was Elsie again, needing to tell me something, so I reached for the phone and opened the text message.

CLAY: You still awake?

CLAY: I'd like to talk…we need to talk

CLAY: I'll even come get you if you want…that way we can talk in person. I think this is an in-person conversation to be honest instead of a virtual one. Let me know. I'm close to your brothers. I'll give you ten minutes to get back to me. If I don't hear from you, we can plan something before you leave.

I tapped the edge of my phone, a feeling of anxiousness and excitement building inside of me.

> PEYTON: Hey. I can meet you outside in five minutes.

Almost immediately, those three little dots jumped around, and then my phone vibrated.

> CLAY: I'll meet you two houses down. Don't want to take a chance on waking anyone.

I got up out of bed and quickly slipped out of my pajamas and into a pair of yoga pants and a sweater. I pulled my hair up into a clip and slipped from my bedroom. I could see the light on under Knox and Lorelai's door, and I could hear the TV on in my mother's room. They were all still awake. Once past their rooms, I tiptoed around the corner into the kitchen and jumped when I saw movement out of the corner of my eye.

"My god…Lorelai, you scared me," I said, placing my hand on my chest.

"I'm sorry," she whispered. "I thought everyone was asleep. Are you going somewhere?" she asked, looking at me, noticing my purse in my hands.

"I was just going to take a walk. Needed my bag for my phone so I can listen to music," I lied.

"Oh, okay. Is everything okay?" she questioned, taking me in with a curious expression.

I nodded. "Yeah, of course. Just wanted to get a little air and walk off dinner." I smiled.

"Well, make sure you take a coat. It's cool out. Don't go too far, and if you want a ride home, just message me and I'll come get you."

"Thanks, but I won't go far. I'll stay in the neighborhood."

"Oh wait, before you go. Here's my key," she said, grabbing her keys and handing them to me. "Just put them back on the counter when you're back. That way, I won't have to bother you in the morning when I leave for work."

"Thanks," I said, heading toward the door and slipping my shoes on. I turned back to see her take a plate of cut-up fruit, cheese and crackers along with two glasses of water down the hall.

I opened the door, pulling it closed behind me and locking it, then I took off down the driveway and made my way to the house two doors down from where Knox and Lorelai lived, and waited.

I SLIPPED my shoes off and then my jacket and hung it on the hook on the back of the door to Clay's place.

"Take a seat in the living room. I'm going to grab us a couple of bottles of water, a little snack, and I'll be right in," he said, waiting until I turned and made my way into his dimly lit living room.

I sat down on the couch, in the same spot I'd sat that very first night that had started this entire thing. My mind drifted to the memory of us together, and I pulled my legs up under me, grabbing one of the side cushions, hugging it to me. This was my comfort position, one I'd always resorted to when I needed comfort.

I sat there, quietly, looking out at the city lights. There was something so peaceful about being way up high in this city, I thought to myself. If only being this high up could take me far away from the problem that I was currently facing.

"Here you are," Clay said, coming into the living room with a plate of crackers and cheese, some apple slices, grapes, and two bottles of water.

"Thanks," I said, taking the bottle of water from him, watching as he placed the plate down on the table in front of us, then sat down beside me.

I took a sip of water at the same time he took one and then placed the bottle on the table, looking over at him. I was expecting to see anger, but he seemed at peace, as if he wasn't the least bit worried about anything. It always amazed me how some people could be that way.

"So, how long have you known?" he asked.

It was just like Clay to jump right to the point. I mean, he told me he didn't dance around things; when he wanted to know something, he'd ask. He certainly didn't lie about that.

"I found out once I returned from Vermont. So, I've only known for a couple of days. I haven't even seen my doctor yet."

Clay nodded and averted his eyes from mine. He leaned forward and grabbed an apple slice, popping it into his mouth.

"Can I ask you something?" he questioned.

I nodded.

"Am I the father?" he asked, raising his eyes to mine.

"I'm thinking the baby is yours, but until I know how far along I am, I am not sure I can really answer that."

"I see," he said, getting up off the couch, moving to the window, looking out over the city.

He shoved his hands in his pockets as he stood there, rocking back and forth on his feet. I'd never seen Clay this quiet, or this wrapped up in his thoughts. He had always seemed so sure of himself, like he always knew what it was he wanted.

"You've been with Tor since we were together?"

"No, not since we were together, but I was with Tor about five weeks before you, so until I know for sure how far along—"

"Fair enough," he said, holding out his hand for me to stop. "Please don't feel you need to explain anything else. It's not like we were together or anything."

I swallowed hard, unsure what he meant by that. I felt I needed to explain and make sure he knew I hadn't been with anyone but him since the first time we'd been together.

"What did you want to do about this?" he questioned, not giving me a chance to ask him anything or to comment on his last comment.

I thought for a moment.

"I mean, if it is mine, what do you want to do about this? Obviously, if it isn't mine, then I won't have any say…"

"I don't know. I mean, it's all so fresh. I've barely even grasped the idea that I am pregnant, so trying to decide what should happen is almost surreal to me at this point."

"You're telling me," He muttered.

"What does that mean?" I asked, feeling my emotions piling up.

Clay sat down beside me and ran his fingers

through his hair. "I guess it means I'm shocked as well. This wasn't exactly in my plans."

"You think it was in mine?" I questioned, feeling tears building.

"I didn't mean that," Clay said.

"Then what did you mean by it?"

He grew quiet as he sat there, staring ahead. I could tell his mind was going a mile a minute, as mine had been ever since I found out. I focused on breathing while I waited for him to respond. The last thing I needed was to have some sort of panic attack.

"Peyton, I don't know why I said that. I guess I'm just as shocked as you are, maybe even a little more so. I keep playing the first night we spent together over in my mind, the one time, the only time, I ever slipped inside a woman without a condom, and this happens. My entire world has flipped upside down in a matter of about three minutes."

"Your world? Are you suggesting mine hasn't? Hell, it was already bad enough, what with everything that's gone on in the past few months. Now, with the talk of moving here, or more like Knox forcing us, this was the absolute last thing I needed. So, if you think it's only your world that has turned upside down because of this, you're wrong." I sniffled. "Oh, and just so you know, I didn't tell you to make you feel you had to be involved. I didn't tell you to make you feel trapped, either. So, if you don't want to be involved, even if it is your baby, that is okay. I'd just rather you tell me now."

"Peyton, that isn't what I meant," he said, his voice a little louder this time than before.

"It's fine, Clay. I think I'm going to go." I sniffled, getting up off the couch and heading toward the door.

"I'd prefer if we talked this through, Peyton."

"Why, so you can sit here and regret the time we were together and make me feel as if I was just a mistake?"

"Whoa! First, I never said that our time together was a mistake. Don't put words in my mouth."

"Well, from the moment I told you, the only look on your face was one of sickness and worry. You don't even know if it's your baby yet, and without even opening your mouth, you've already let me know you aren't happy about any of this. It's not a wonder my brother has always been adamant about me not getting involved with players from the team."

"Peyton, please. I'm shocked, nothing more."

"Try being me," I cried. "Think about what it's been like for me. I've taken six tests, all of which shoved those two pink lines in my face each time. I had no one to call. I have no one I can go to. No one knows we've been together, aside from the pair of us. I already know if I go to my brother, he'll just be all high and mighty and say I told you so."

"Peyton, I never said I would not be here for you. What about your mom and Lorelai."

I stopped, my eyes falling to the floor.

"They know, don't they?" he questioned.

I slowly nodded. "Mom figured it out before I told her."

"Have they told your brother?"

"No, Mom probably thinks it's Tors. Other than that, she didn't really say much."

"Well, if she knows and Lorelai knows, then why did you come to me? Especially when you really don't know if it's mine or not."

"Oh my god, are you seriously standing there and asking me that?" I cried.

"I am."

I paced back and forth across his living room, anger and hurt building inside of me. "It's almost like you think I only fucked you to get back at my brother. I came to you for support. If it's yours, I wanted you there, but only because you want to be, not because you're being forced to be here."

"Dammit, Peyton, calm down, would you? I'm entitled to my feelings, just like you are. I'm navigating this as well, and for the love of God, don't put words in my mouth."

I stared at him. I could see the anger on his face.

He didn't need to say anything else. I spun around and made my way to the living room door.

"Where are you going?"

"I'm leaving. Maybe we can talk another time, when I've found the answers I need, or better yet, the answers you need, then we can take it from there," I said, slipping my shoes on and grabbing my jacket.

"Peyton, I don't want you to leave."

"That's too bad. I'm leaving."

"Give me a minute then and I'll take you home," Clay said, walking to the door, slipping his shoe on. "I don't want you walking across the city alone at night."

"No need. I wouldn't want to put you out. I mean, fun time is all over now, isn't it. I'll just take a cab," I said, pulling the door open and slamming it shut behind me.

Chapter 13

Clay

THE SLAM of the door echoed through my apartment. How the hell had things escalated so fast? The last thing I wanted her to do was leave. What I wanted was to pull her into my arms and assure her I'd be there every step of the way, regardless of whose baby it was. Instead, I'd blown that because I'd not been able to take a step back and look at the situation rationally.

It wasn't just the news of a baby that had me feeling off. I'd felt off ever since our first night together. I'd not been able to concentrate on much of anything without the thought of her invading my mind. I'd not understood the excitement I'd felt seeing her in

Vermont that weekend either, or how I felt seeing her earlier tonight after I'd arrived for dinner. These feelings weren't something I was used to.

I'd also struggled with the events from the night I'd run into Sonya, the only woman I'd gone back to time and time again. She lived in Vancouver, so when I needed to blow off steam, she was only a phone call away. It didn't happen often, but when it had, it had always been a good time. Only this time, when I ran into her, something was different. She did absolutely nothing for me. Even her rubbing against me that night, dancing, normally would have made me hard as a damn rock, but nothing. It was as if my cock had broken.

After that, I started wondering if I'd ever be okay again. Then I'd remembered Dylan talking about how he'd felt after he and Aurora had slept together for the first time. They'd shared a one-night stand while on vacation in Mexico, and he'd freaking kicked himself for almost an entire year for not getting her number. All he kept telling us was that no other woman could ever compare to how he'd felt that night with her.

I'd thought he was being ridiculous. I mean, sex was sex, wasn't it? It was all good. Then, when he'd admitted not being able to look at or get aroused by another woman, I thought he was crazy. He claimed he was in love with this one-night stand girl. I'd thought there was something wrong with him. We'd even tried fixing him up with some girls, none of which worked. Now, I was wondering about the same thing.

Was I in love with Peyton? Had she really rocked me that hard in bed that I'd wanted to give up other women and, dare I say, settle down? Was this another Dylan-Aurora situation? I wondered. Was it even possible?

What was I doing? All I knew was that right now, there was no way I could let her leave. Not like this, not upset. There was also no way I was letting her take a fucking cab home. She could either come back upstairs with me and talk this shit through or I was driving her home, and we'd revisit this in a couple of days before she returned to Vermont. Come hell or high water, we were going to figure this shit out.

I should have remained calm, I thought as I took off out the door and down to the lobby. The moment the elevator doors opened, I ran out in time to see that Peyton was already in the back of a cab, pulling the door closed. I ran to the main door and opened it, just to watch the cab pull away.

Running my hands through my hair, I took off back upstairs to my condo where I flopped down on the couch and looked out over the city. As peaceful as the night lights were, my mind was screaming. I really needed my boys—at least one of them—so I grabbed my phone and pulled up what I was certain was the last one of our message threads—the one without Knox. This had to stay away from him. I typed feverishly, re-read the message, and then hit sent.

> CLAY: I have a hypothetical question for you, jerks. Anyone around?

Before I could close the chat, those little dots bounced around. I'd figured they'd all be in bed, but I should have known better. It seemed one of us was always around when we needed one another.

> DYLAN: Shoot

> LEVI: Go for it.

> LUCAS: What's up?

I smiled as those three messages came in at almost the same time.

> CLAY: What would one of you do if, let's say, you got a girl pregnant?

> DYLAN: Have you forgotten? I already have one, and you already know what I've done.

> LUCAS: Uh dude, wish that hell on me. I swear...

CLAY: No Dylan I haven't forgotten, and no Lucas, I'm not wishing it on you. Poor Ella has been through enough, what with marrying you already. I'd never curse that gorgeous girl with something like that.

LUCAS: I'm not sure how to take that? Fellas?

DYLAN: What a dick thing to say...

LEVI: Who are you wishing this on? Better not be me?

CLAY: It's just a hypothetical question.

LUCAS: I don't think so. Who got someone knocked up? Levi, you've been seeing some chick, is it you?

LEVI: Nope, I always wrap it...god how did I even get pulled into this?

LUCAS: Colton

COLTON: What? I'm single as single can be. In fact, I'm wondering if my dick even still works. It's been that long.

LUCAS: Is it Knox?? Is Lorelai pregnant??? We can't have both our therapists off on mat leave at the same time. The team will fall apart. My knee has been acting up again. She's the only one who knows how to treat it.

CLAY: Any therapist can treat a knee...don't panic...

KNOX: WHAT the fuck? Don't you fucks start spreading those types of rumors? Last thing I need is to be pulled into Larson's office, or Thompkins office...

I glanced at my screen, my heart in my throat, when I saw Knox respond. I thought I'd grabbed the chat we'd started when Lucas was in Vegas. As I scrolled back up the screen, I saw I was wrong. I'd grabbed the wrong fucking chat. Panic filled me as I watched the conversation continue to unfold.

DYLAN: No rumor, just hypothetically guessing who might be pregnant.

KNOX: Pregnant? It's your woman, dumbass, in case you haven't noticed.

DYLAN: For the love of god, see what you've started, Clay.

CLAY: I started?

DYLAN: Yeah, it was your
hypothetical…

LEVI: Just spill it….Who'd you
knock up?

COLTON: Clay, You knocked someone
up? Way to go…didn't they teach you
to wrap it before…

DYLAN: Care to share, Harris?

CLAY: I said, HYPOTHETICAL…

KNOX: Is it the girl I heard you with
when we were in Vermont?

I swallowed hard as I stared at the screen. He'd heard me with a girl in Vermont? He'd heard me with Peyton? How the hell had he heard us? I seriously wanted to delete this entire set of messages and go back in time, wishing I'd sent nothing. Instead, they were like a shiver of sharks going after a meal. They wanted the goods, and while I'd tried to play it off as a hypothetical question, I should have known they'd all know it was real.

CLAY: Girl in Vermont?

I figured if I played dumb, I'd at least figure out how the hell he'd heard us.

KNOX: One of the guys mentioned he saw a woman enter your room. I'll admit, at quick glance, he thought it was Peyton, but I know you know better than that. Plus, I'd moved rooms and was put in the room next to yours. FYI, I'm not deaf. Sounded like a hell of a good time though. Just ask Lorelai about our call that night.

DYLAN: WHOA...way too much information that none of us need to know there Evans.

LUCAS: Yeah...didn't need to know that...

LEVI: Kill me now....

COLTON: Why did I need to read that...my eyes will never unsee those words...

DYLAN: However, Clay, this would explain the shitty games you've been playing. Remember how badly I played after I first found out about Aurora being pregnant?

LUCAS: Yeah, you played like shit. Probably exactly how you'll play in a couple of weeks after the baby is born.

DYLAN: Thanks for that.

LUCAS: Just saying it like it is.

CLAY: I haven't been playing like shit and seriously, it was hypothetical.

KNOX: Fine, provided I was in a relationship, I'd be excited as fuck. If I wasn't, I'd probably be getting in touch with my lawyer, you know, to cover my ass from her. She could take all my damn money for support, hypothetically speaking, of course.

COLTON: Same

LUCAS: So, if I were to get someone pregnant, it would be Ella, so I have no worries.

DYLAN: Already there, and you already know what I did.

LEVI: Hypothetically, I'd be finding some new friends. The advice in here sucks.

KNOX: That too...but seriously, if you need to get a lawyer.

COLTON: Who was the broad you shacked up with that night?

LEVI: Yeah?

LUCAS: It really looked like Peyton from far away...

KNOX: Drop that now, Lucas. It's my sister you're talking about and besides, she already told me it wasn't her.

I squirmed at the last comment. He'd asked his sister. Jesus, I could only imagine how she must have felt during that interrogation, because I knew Knox well enough to know it wouldn't just be a question. It would also come with a lecture.

CLAY: Didn't catch her name and I don't need a fucking lawyer. Jesus, it was a hypothetical.

I placed my phone on the table and ran my fingers through my hair. They'd been absolutely no help. All I'd wanted was an answer to my question, I thought to myself as my phone continued to ping with unread messages.

Finally, I reached for my phone, going to turn the ringer off, when I glanced at the screen. There was a private message from Dylan there while the conversation between the guys continued.

DYLAN: Is everything okay? Are you in some trouble? It will stay between us.

I knew without a doubt he'd keep it between us, but I was still a little hesitant to say anything. There normally wasn't anything I wouldn't tell these guys. This time, it was only different because of who the girl was. Otherwise, it wouldn't have been a hypothetical question at all and I'd have spilled it all.

CLAY: You're sure?

DYLAN: I've spilled nothing you've ever told me. No reason to start now.

CLAY: It can't leave this chat, I'm serious. I regret even starting the other chat. It was a stupid move on my part.

DYLAN: That's fine. It will stay between us and won't be revealed unless you do it yourself.

CLAY: It's Peyton.

As I hit enter, I closed my eyes, instantly regretting

telling him. I pinched the bridge of my nose, waiting for a reply.

DYLAN: Peyton?

DYLAN: ...As in Evans?

CLAY: Yep.

DYLAN: Holllleeeee... fuck... me....

DYLAN: Please, for the love of your actual hockey stick, tell me this is hypothetical????

CLAY: No, this... is...real life...

DYLAN: *whistles*

CLAY: I know...I'm a walking dead man

DYLAN: you're certain?

CLAY: Yep...she told me tonight

DYLAN: How? When?

CLAY: Started six weeks ago…I ran into her at The Tilted Flask the night I was supposed to meet up with the guys. Some creep was hitting on her, so I stepped in. One thing led to another…

DYLAN: My god, no wonder you were quiet tonight.

CLAY: I didn't know what else to do. It's bad enough I've been so off my game because of her.

DYLAN: Are you saying all the shitty playing has been because of her?

CLAY: Yes, since the first night I've not been able to get her off my mind.

DYLAN: So before you got the news?

CLAY: Yep…

DYLAN: Okay…don't panic. Leave it with me, let me sleep on it.

CLAY: Please, don't mention this to Aurora. I'm sure Lorelai will tell her in time.

DYLAN: Lorelai knows?

CLAY: Yep...and Reese...

DYLAN: and Knox doesn't?

CLAY: I'm still alive...

DYLAN: Don't worry. She owns me, but what you and I talked about here will never be disclosed and the conversation will be deleted from my phone once the conversation is done. Best to be safe.

CLAY: Thanks man...please come up with something...

DYLAN: One question: do you want to be involved? That might change how I answer your question.

CLAY: I don't know if she even wants me to be a part of anything. Peyton came over here tonight and we tried to talk things through, but I acted like an ass. She's scared and feels very alone...and before I knew it everything went to shit, and she left.

CLAY: Honestly, I'd like to be involved very much but only if she wants me to be.

DYLAN: So you have a thing for her...

CLAY: More than a thing...to be
honest, I've never felt this way about a
woman before...

DYLAN: When did that happen?

CLAY: The first night I spent with her...
she blew my fucking mind...

DYLAN: I get it, no need to explain
that to me.

CLAY: Didn't think so.

DYLAN: I'm gonna get some sleep,
come up with an answer for you and
take it from there

CLAY: Thanks man.

DYLAN: You're welcome. Oh, and
don't worry, we'll get it worked out.

CLAY: Thanks, I knew I could count on
one of you...

DYLAN: Always.

I sat there for a moment, feeling a little better than
I had a few moments ago. I got up, shut the lights off,

and wandered down the hall to my bedroom. I threw my phone on the charger and then crawled into bed.

I lay there, staring at the ceiling. The only thing on my mind right now was Peyton. God, I wished I'd kept a level head earlier. Instead of her being back in her room alone at Knox and Lorelai's, she could have been here in my bed, wrapped in my arms, where she should be anyway.

"Fuck it," I muttered to myself and reached for my phone.

I quickly opened the chat she and I had going between the two of us.

> CLAY: Just so you know, if the baby is mine, I will be there with you every single step of the way. You aren't alone in this and I'm only going to tell you that once. I'm also going to say that tonight, I was an idiot. I'm sorry.

The moment I hit send, I felt a little better. At least she now knew how I felt. It would be up to her what she did with that information.

I placed my phone back down on the charger, placed my hands behind my head, and closed my eyes. Morning came early, practice came earlier and so did tomorrow night's game. One that was far too important for the team to lose.

Chapter 14

Peyton

WHEN I WOKE up this morning, I'd seen Clay's message from last night and immediately I wanted to see him, but they were at practice and then gearing up for tonight's game. I didn't want to distract him from what I knew was important.

I didn't respond to his message. Instead, I'd waited until everyone had left for the game, then I left a note letting Mom, Lorelai, and Knox know I was going out with some friends and wouldn't be back until morning. I'd come to Clay's building and waited outside until someone came along and I could sneak in. I took off to his floor and parked myself in the hallway, waiting for him to come home.

I glanced at my watch. It was just after eleven. The game finished half an hour ago. They'd won, allowing them to advance to the second round of the playoffs. Part of me had wished I'd gone to watch them play, so I could be a part of the excitement.

I jumped when I heard Clay's voice coming down the hall. I quickly got up, brushing off my pants and straightening my shirt. I knew Knox had to head straight home after the game because he was taking my mom to see another condo early in the morning, so I knew he wouldn't be with Clay.

As the voices got closer, I looked up in time to see Clay and Dylan coming down the hall, neither one of them noticing me at first. They were laughing and talking about the game, and then Dylan made eye contact with me. It was then Clay looked up, surprised at seeing me here.

"Peyton? How long have you been—"

"I…I shouldn't have come," I said, wanting to bolt as Dylan stood there looking between the two of us.

"Clay, how about I see you in the morning?" Dylan said, placing his hand on his shoulder.

Clay nodded, still looking in my direction. "Sure thing. Thanks for the lift."

"No problem. Peyton, good to see you, as always,"

Dylan said, before he turned and made his way back toward the elevator.

"What are you doing here?" Clay asked, pulling his keys from his pocket and slipping one into the lock.

"It was stupid of me to come without warning you. Fuck, now my brother is going to—"

"Don't worry, Dylan won't say anything. Come on in," he said, holding the door with one hand and waiting for me as I looked down the hall in the direction Dylan had gone.

"How do you know that?" I asked, still looking down the hall in the direction Dylan had gone.

"Trust me, okay. I know. Come on."

I walked into Clay's apartment and waited while he shut and locked the door.

"Here, give me your coat," he said, waiting while I slipped out of it. He hung both our jackets in the closet and then placed his hand on my lower back, guiding me into his living room.

"Want something to drink?" he questioned as I took a seat on his couch.

I nodded and watched as he made his way to the fridge, where he grabbed two bottles of water and returned, sitting down beside me.

Immediately, we both spoke, only for us both to stop and smile at one another.

"Go ahead," he urged, taking my bottle of water and cracking the lid for me.

"Thank you. I got your message this morning. I thought it would be best if I came to see you instead of messaging.

"I'm glad you did. I've been wanting to talk to you as well. First, I want to say I am sorry for panicking yesterday."

"No, it's okay. I don't blame you. I wasn't exactly calm myself."

"It's understandable," he said, placing his hand on my upper thigh and squeezing.

I looked down at his hand, then met his eyes, placing my hand on top of his.

"You really want to be a part of this?" I questioned.

He nodded, his eyes on mine, before they fell to my lips. "I do," he whispered, leaning forward, his lips grazing mine. "I don't want to miss a thing."

A wave of warmth filled me as I leaned forward, meeting his lips. I closed my eyes as he ran his hand through my hair. I shifted on the couch, kneeling on the couch as he sat back a bit, tapping my hip.

I straddled his lap, just like I'd done the first night, resting my hands on his shoulders, and leaned forward, kissing him as his hands travelled down my back, until they were resting on my ass. He gripped my cheeks as he kissed me deeper.

I could have gotten lost in his kiss, but all I could wonder was how he was going to be a part of everything when I was going back to Vermont in a couple of days. I placed my hands on his chest and broke the kiss.

"What is it?" he asked, knowing something was on my mind.

"This is how we got into this mess." I giggled.

"Uh-huh, I know."

His eyes met mine, studying them. "What else?"

"Clay, how is that going to work, though? You're here…and I'll be back in Vermont in a couple of days."

"You mentioned something about you moving here."

"Yes, but—"

"No buts. Until then, I'll be there when I can. Most of it for now will have to be via text or video chat, at least until the season is over. I'll try to be available whenever you need me to be, minus game time and practice, of course, but once you are back…"

"Once I'm back, what? Once I'm back, I'm sure my mother will have told my brother and I'll be under lock and key. You'll never get near me."

He smiled. "Peyton, I'm not afraid of your mother.

She actually likes me, and I'm sure it will be a relief for her to know that it isn't Tor's, and as for your brother, he's going to have to face the fact that you aren't a kid, and that shit happens between two consenting adults."

"Try telling him that."

"I plan on it. I'll take his beating, I'll take his words, but he's the one who is going to have to face the fact that I..."

Clay stopped speaking and swallowed hard as he looked at me.

"That what?" I questioned, watching him as he now averted his eyes.

When he said nothing, I placed my hand on his cheek and turned his head toward me.

"Clay…what is it?"

He swallowed hard, then licked his lips before raising his eyes to mine.

"Peyton, you need to know that I haven't been able to get you out of my mind. Ever since the first night we were together. What you told me should really have scared the hell out of me, but once you left last night, I realized it was more a leg jerk reaction than truthfully being scared."

"Really?"

He nodded and smiled softly.

"Once I realized it, all I wanted to do was hold you and have you here by my side. I felt like an absolute piece of shit knowing you were at your brother's, alone and scared."

My body flooded with heat as I leaned forward and wrapped my arms around him.

"Please, you don't need to feel like a piece of shit. I probably should have handled things a little differently. I'm used to being with guys—"

He placed his fingers on my lips, stopping me from going any further, the look in his eyes so intense and full of need.

"You aren't with those guys anymore, Peyton. You're with me now, if you'll have me. I'll never treat you as a second option. From here on out, you are my main priority. I'll do anything for you, and I hope I'll never let down."

I could feel my eyes burning at his admission. In less than six weeks, I'd gone from having someone who treated me like garbage, who stole, cheated, and lied to me, to a man who sat here, wanting me to be a part of his life and wanting to be a part of mine.

When I felt the tears slide down my cheeks, he brushed them away with his thumb before meeting my lips with his. Then, with his arms wrapped securely around me, he lifted not only himself but me as well from the couch and carried me down the hall to his bedroom, just the way he had the very first night I'd been here.

He kicked the door closed behind us and carried me over to the bed where he put me down. Without a word, he walked over to his dresser, opened one of his drawers, and pulled out a Dominator's T-shirt, and gently tossed it to me.

"For you." He smiled.

"For me? I don't understand."

I was certain he was bringing me down here for sex, only when he turned to look my way, I saw none of that in his eyes.

"Yes, for you, to wear to bed. It's late. You need your rest, I need mine, and I want you to spend the night in my arms."

I watched as he headed toward his closet. It felt weird that he didn't want to have sex. I'd never spent the night with any guy without sex. Actually, that was the only time I was in their bed. After that, they'd drive me home and drop me off, or they'd simply leave.

I sat down on the edge of his bed and slipped my jeans off, neatly folding them and placing them on the floor, then slipped my shirt over my head, removed my bra, and then slipped the shirt he'd given me over my head.

"I'll be right out," he muttered, and I turned to see him enter the bathroom, returning only a couple of minutes later. "There is a new toothbrush on the counter for you, along with a set of towels for you in the morning."

He pulled back the covers on his side of the bed and crawled in. I sat there, unsure of what to do. This was a foreign concept to me. When I felt his hand on my hip, I glanced over my shoulder at him.

"Are you getting in?"

I stood up and went to pull back the blankets, but he beat me to it. He tapped the mattress, waiting for me to slip in. I crawled in and laid down while he dropped the covers on me, then slipped his arm under my neck and slid up against me, resting his arm around my waist.

"Comfortable?" he asked quietly before placing a kiss on the side of my neck.

The heat from his body enveloped me. I closed my eyes and placed my hand on top of his.

"Very," I answered, allowing my body to sink into the soft mattress while welcoming his warmth.

I could feel him move away and was about to say something when the light went out, bathing the room in darkness. I felt him pull me a little into the centre of the bed, against his body.

"You warm enough?"

"Yes."

"You're sure, because you are shaking."

Yep, I was, there was no denying it, but it wasn't

because I was cold. It was because I'd never in my life been treated this way, and I wasn't sure how to react.

"I know, I'm sorry…"

"Don't be sorry. Is something wrong?"

I was quiet. How was I going to tell him this was new to me, so new that I didn't know how to react. Maybe I should have just come out with it, be more like Clay, say what was on my mind.

"Can I share something with you?"

"Of course. No secrets with us."

"I've never been treated this way before."

"What way?" he questioned, rubbing my shoulder as he pulled me a little closer.

"Spending the night without being expected to…"

I could feel his body tense. He rolled up onto his arm, and I could see him looking down at me.

"Peyton, I'm so sorry that has been what you've gotten to think is acceptable," he said, looking down into my eyes. "Please, from now on, I want you to remember that part of your life is over. If there is ever anything you don't want to do in any aspect of our relationship, especially in this bedroom, there will never be questions asked.

"As for tonight, this is what I want right now. I need this, and I think this is what you need as well. You need to know that I am here for you, and I want to let you know I am here for you without the confusion of adding sex to it. Sex complicates things, and it's not the way I want to deal with our situation. That doesn't mean I don't want to either, so before you get too far into your own head and start thinking that I am not interested, know I am interested."

I couldn't help it as more tears slid down my cheeks as he pressed his lips to mine in the most tender kiss I'd ever experienced in my life. Somehow, I knew without a doubt in my heart that Clay meant every word he'd said, and the moment he wrapped his arms around me, I knew this was where I wanted to be, regardless of the flack I was sure would come our way.

Chapter 15

Clay - Wednesday

"Any news yet?" Dylan asked, sitting down on the bench next to me while we both took a break after completing our drills.

I glanced down at my phone and shook my head as we watched the rest of the guys on the team still going.

Peyton had been back in Vermont for a few days now, and I knew that today was the day she had her doctor's appointment. In fact, she was probably in the office right now, I thought to myself, noticing the time.

"Not yet, but she told me she'd message me right away once the appointment was over."

"How did the other night go?" Dylan questioned, squirting water into his mouth.

Dylan and I had talked in the car the other night when he'd driven me home after the game. He was going to come in, have some food, and talk a little more about how I should go about breaking the news to Knox. I firmly believed I should be the one to tell him. As I'd told Peyton, I'd take his hits, I'd take his words, and then I'd prove to him I was there for her. She shouldn't be the one to shoulder the brunt of that. Dylan had apparently devised a plan, but then we'd found Peyton in the hall, so he'd left. I had mentioned nothing about how things had gone between the two of us.

"Went well. I made sure I let her know I wanted to be part of things. Then she spent the night at my place. I am worried though. I'm not sure what sort of guys she's been with, but it bothered me she was more nervous just to lie in my arms than she was the first time we'd slept together. She admitted to me she wasn't used to being with someone in that capacity, where they didn't want sex. Makes me wonder if Knox even knows the type of guys she's been with."

"Probably not, or maybe he does. I can't say. All I know is that he's fought with her frequently to get her away from the ones she'd been dating. Which makes me think he knows the truth about how she'd been being treated. Although I'd have thought that these guys would be a little worse for wear."

"No doubt."

Dylan cleared his throat just as the guys came off the ice, all piling into the area. I glanced at my phone again, anticipation building inside of me.

"Harris, what the hell is so important?" Coach Thompkins questioned, as he stood in front of us, prepared to give us one of his usual lectures. "You haven't stopped looking at that damn thing all morning, which is why they aren't supposed to be at practice."

The guys all turned and looked in my direction. They all waited as I shifted on the bench, the conversation I'd started the other night surely in the forefront of their minds.

"Just hypothetically speaking, of course," Colton said, causing them all to chuckle.

"Sorry, coach, I'm just waiting for some news."

"What sort of news?" Levi questioned. "Hypothetical news or actual news?"

Each one of them was now watching me, trying not to laugh as I glanced at them, then cleared my throat again before taking a drink of water.

"I'm waiting to find out if I'm going to be a father," I muttered.

It was then I felt a pat on the shoulder and looked up to see Knox standing behind me.

"Congratulations, man. I did not know. I mean,

after the conversation the other night, I'll admit I was wondering, but seriously, that's fantastic. Who's the lucky lady?"

All the guys looked at me, waiting for me to answer. Instead, I just shrugged.

"I'm going to wait to announce that once I know for a fact that it's happening."

"Alright, fair enough," Knox muttered.

"Okay, well, Harris, congrats. Now, men, let's get down to business," Coach Thompkins said, waiting while we all took a seat.

I'D JUST LEFT the treatment room after having a massage and was on my way back to the locker room, where I planned to take a hot shower. I'd checked my phone before my appointment and again the moment the therapist had left the room, but there was still nothing from Peyton.

I was starting to worry as I entered the locker room; the place was quiet. I walked over to my locker and began pulling out my stuff for my shower when my phone finally went off. I grabbed it and relief flooded me when I saw Peyton's name. Opening our chat, I read her message.

> PEYTON: Sorry the Doctor was running behind. I wanted to let you know that the test results were correct. I'm approximately four weeks along. Call me tonight when you are home after the game. I have to run to school to see about getting a transfer and then get into work for a meeting with my boss, besides I know you are probably at the arena.

I was about to respond when the door to the locker room opened and in walked Knox and the rest of the guys. Immediately, I shut my phone down and dumped it into my locker.

"Well, big guy…any news?" Knox questioned, smiling.

I turned around and met Dylan's gaze. The rest of the guys were already digging through their lockers, and he subtly shook his head. I could tell from the look on his face he was warning me that now probably wasn't the best time to say anything, but for whatever reason, I didn't heed his warning. I really needed to get this out in the open because it was literally killing me to be lying to one of my best friends.

"Knox, we need to talk."

The rest of the guys froze and slowly turned around, looking in my direction as Knox stopped what he was searching for in his bag and glanced over his shoulder at me.

"What for?" he questioned, a smile on his face that slowly washing away the longer he looked at me.

The guys all froze to their spots as they stared at the pair of us.

"Why exactly should we talk, Clay?" he questioned, straightening up to his full height, turning his body to me.

I struggled to find my words as he stared at me. No one ever could grasp how Knox could be one of the scariest guys on the team until they were in my position. Then and only then would they understand.

"I asked you a question," he said, crossing his arms.

I looked around the room, praying something would come to my mind to ease the tension in the room. I wanted to say something lighthearted and funny, but again, I came up with nothing.

"Knox, I…"

It was then his eyes grew wide, and he dropped his arms, his fists clenching at his sides. "So help you…" He yelled, "PEYTON?"

The guys all watched in horror as Knox crossed the room and grabbed hold of me by the shirt. I couldn't deny it, and I wasn't about to fight one of my best friends. I'd done the deed, and just like I'd told Peyton,

I'd take the lumps that were to come with it if need be. Apparently, they need be.

"Oh hell, is he going to kill him?" I heard Levi mutter. "What do we do?"

The room was silent as Knox stared at me, his arm cocked back, ready to beat me.

"It's Peyton."

"God, you fucker," Knox said through clenched teeth, his jaw tighter than I'd ever seen it. "How could you do this?"

"Knox, before you get angry—"

"Little too late for that, don't you think?" he gritted.

"Look, I didn't mean for it to happen. In fact, I was only trying to save her from making a huge mistake," I said, looking him directly in the eyes.

I wasn't lying. That was all I'd intended to do. To save her from getting with that guy, and I'd accomplished that, but I'd also accomplished the results that I now faced, and while I'd had no intention of doing that, it had somehow happened.

"You didn't mean for it to happen?" he repeated, staring at me.

"Exactly. I didn't mean for it to happen the first time, and I certainly didn't expect for it to happen again."

"Exactly how many times has it *happened*?" he asked, emphasizing the word it.

I wasn't sure I should answer that now that I knew he'd heard us in Vermont.

"Wait a minute…"

I could see that Knox had already figured it out. I didn't need to say another word.

"Knox…" I mumbled.

"You mean to tell me it was her I listened to moan and cry that night in Vermont as you banged the hell out of her?" he yelled, frantic.

He gripped my shirt tighter, and I already knew there was no getting it out it, his fist was coming directly for my face. Then I felt the hit, and another.

"Grab him!" I heard someone shout as Knox let go of my shirt and I fell against the lockers.

A searing pain ripped through my ribs as Knox kicked me in the side, taking my breath away.

I was expecting another hit but heard a scuffle and Knox swearing to let him go. I opened my eyes and saw Dylan and Colton holding Knox up against the lockers. Levi and Lucas came over to me and helped me up off the floor.

"Knox, calm down. Don't do something you're going to regret," Dylan said, holding his arm.

"Yeah, man, it's not worth it. Let's just get out of here and calm you down," Colton added.

"Dylan, Colton, let go of me and stay the hell out of it! He's getting what he deserves—"

"I won't stay out of it. Clay seriously didn't mean for this to happen. He's taking it seriously…and he's trying to do what is right."

"Oh right, the playboy, the manwhore of the group, is taking this seriously. Right!" Knox yelled. It was then he realized what Dylan was saying and stopped, looking over at him. "How do you know he's taking it seriously?" he questioned, thinking it through. "Wait, you knew?" he questioned.

Dylan looked at Colton but said nothing. He just stood there, staring back at Knox.

"You fucking knew, and you didn't come to me? What about you, Colton, did you know too?"

"I know shit," Colton said, holding his hands up.

Knox turned back to Dylan, shoving him in the chest, throwing him right into the bank of lockers behind him, turning his sights on him instead of me.

"I did, but Clay asked me to keep it under wraps," Dylan argued, trying not to be confrontational.

"What kind of fucking friend are you?" Knox yelled, glaring at Dylan. Then he turned and looked at me. "You…you're dead to me, and don't you even dare think about coming near me, or my family, especially Peyton, ever again? Do so and you'll find the fuck out.

I should have your ass kicked right off this fucking team for what you've done…"

He whipped around, slamming his locker door shut and took off out of the room. The entire room was quiet as we all stood there looking at one another, the tension still thick in the air.

Chapter 16

Peyton

I LAY IN BED, trying to force myself to stay awake. I watched the game. Clay hadn't played tonight, which was odd, yet I knew he was there because I'd seen him skate onto the ice at the start.

I glanced over at the clock on my side table—a little after eleven. I was certain the guys would be back home by now. They normally were when they played a home game. I picked up my phone and checked to see if I had any messages, but there was nothing.

I rolled onto my side and closed my eyes. I felt uneasy all afternoon, especially after the doctor's appointment. I'd given my notice at work and then had come home and started packing. Mom had let me know she'd finally found a place and that she had told William that the money he'd received from Knox for this month's rent would be the last.

I let out a sigh and rolled onto my back when my phone rang. Grabbing it, I brought the phone up to my ear.

"Hey, how are you doing??" Clay's voice asked over the phone.

"Okay, you?" I asked.

"Tired. It's been a day. Did you watch the game?"

"I did. I noticed you didn't play tonight," I said, bunching the corner of my sheets in my hand as I lay in bed, staring up at the ceiling.

"Nah, not tonight," he muttered. "Doctor's appointment went well?" he asked, changing the subject.

I frowned. I didn't like that he hadn't expanded on the reason he hadn't played. Clay only ever stepped out of the game when injured or sick. I knew that much from my brother.

"Yeah, how did you feel about the news?"

I'd been worried about telling him how far along I'd been through a text message. I'd wanted to see his face when I told him the news. That way I could gauge his reaction myself, because I still feared somewhere inside, he wasn't serious about being there for me.

"I'd planned to be there for you no matter what. Even if it wasn't mine," he said, going quiet for a few moments before clearing his throat. "What I'd like to know is how you see this going?"

"What do you mean?" I questioned, not sure what it was he wanted to know.

"Well, what do you want? Did you want to try to co-parent, or do you want to be together?"

I knew what I'd always wanted if I were to have children with someone, but I certainly didn't want to force him to want the same things. However, I knew I needed to be honest with him instead of dancing around the subject or trying to hint or maybe never tell him what it was I wanted. This wasn't just me I was messing with. I had someone else to think about now, which totally blew my mind when I thought about it.

"To be honest, I always thought that when I had kids, or was lucky enough to have them, I'd be with the father, in a solid relationship."

I swallowed hard when the line went quiet. It stayed quiet for a few minutes.

"When are you coming back out here?" he asked. "Maybe we should try to settle things?"

"I'll be out this coming weekend," I answered.

"Okay, that sounds good."

Once again, he went quiet. I wanted to see him, to see his expression.

"Clay, before I go to sleep, do you think we could video chat?" I asked.

Clay cleared his throat. "I don't know if that is a good idea right now," he said.

"Why?" I questioned, fear running through me. He hadn't played tonight…now he didn't want to video chat.

Then, as if he could read my mind, the line went dead, and my phone rang, a video chat invite popping up.

I pulled up the video call and then saw the reason Clay hadn't wanted to be on video. The cut across the bridge of his nose was red and bloody, but the swollen shut black eye and bruising were horrific.

"What the hell happened to you?" I cried, horrified.

Clay chuckled a little. "Don't freak out, but your brother happened."

Tears came to my eyes first because of the damage Knox had caused, and then for another reason. "Why would he have done that?" I questioned; positive I knew the answer already.

"I told him," Clay answered. "About us."

"What?" I questioned, panic filling me.

"I told him today. I couldn't keep it from him any longer. Like I told you, I was prepared to take what was coming my way."

"God…I'm going to let him have it," I said, anger rising in me.

"No, you aren't. We are going to let him cool off, and then we are going to deal with him like the adults we are. He'll come around. I am sure it was just a shock to him. Now, I'm going to get some ice on my face so I don't miss any other games and get to bed. I want you to do the same, and I will see you on the weekend."

"But, Clay, he can't do this—"

"It's done, Peyton. He did it and I expected it. Don't worry, he'll be fine."

"I'm not worried about him."

"Peyton, we'll be fine," Clay said, the confidence in his voice reassuring me. "Now, go get some rest and I'll see you in a few days."

I WAS JUST PLACING the load of towels I'd washed into the dryer and started it when my cell phone rang. I glanced at the screen to see my brother's name. Swearing under my breath, I contemplated not answering it but then reconsidered. I was pissed with him, and he needed to know it. How dare he hit Clay.

"What?" I barked into the phone, not caring how I started this entire conversation between the two of us.

"Don't you dare start off a conversation like that with me. I'm beyond pissed with you!" Knox yelled.

I could hear Mom or Lorelai in the background muttering something, but he covered the mouthpiece and mumbled something at them.

I had nothing to say because he had no right to be angry at me. I was an adult, and if I wanted to have a relationship with Clay, I had every right to.

"I see you have nothing to say. That figures, it's very much like you. I don't know why I ever expected anything different from you, Peyton."

Tears filled my eyes as he spoke. His tone was harsh, his words even more so.

"What do you mean by that?"

"God, you sat right there that night and lied to my face in Vermont. I asked you point-blank if you were in his room and you fucking lied to me."

"That's because it wasn't any of your business."

"Not my business?"

"That's right, you heard me. It's not your business."

"Seriously, Peyton, of all the guys on the team, Clay?"

I frowned. Was he upset about the fact that I'd

messed around with one guy on the team or was he more upset at the fact that it was Clay?

"What is that supposed to mean? I would imagine it would upset you regardless of who it was that I messed around with."

"Correct, but Clay?"

"Yes, Knox, Clay. What's the problem?"

"It's Clay, manwhore of the team. Jesus, if you even knew how many women—"

"Knox, it's none of my concern, and it's not like you are a saint, either. Hell, I'm sure you've had your fun just as much as any of the others on the team."

"Peyton, this isn't about me and my fun. This is about you and your choices and—"

"It's always about me and my choices, isn't it? Well, my choice was Clay, Knox, like it or not. It honestly didn't even start out being that way. I ran into him the night you forced me to face the security after I shoplifted."

"What are you talking about? The night you lied about being at my place tucked into bed, the night you came home drunk and staggered down the hallway… that night?"

How had he known? He'd been asleep when I'd left, I was certain of it, and I'd been as quiet as a mouse, or so I thought when I returned.

"Yes, that night."

"So, you've been fucking him this entire time?"

"No, I never said that. If you really need to know, I slept with him when you forced Mom and I to go to Vancouver after I called you. I was in trouble that night. I'd stopped into some little dive bar there and some guy was trying to pick me up. He was touching me and saying all these things, making me feel not only uncomfortable but super dirty. I didn't know how to handle it, and then I saw Clay across the room. He'd promised me that if ever I needed anything and you weren't around, I could count on any of the guys on the team."

"Oh, I see how it is. You were horned up and wanted to get laid."

"You are impossible. No. I needed help. He came over and chased the other guy away. We talked for quite a long time after that, and then one thing led to another. We're attracted to one another, and it just sort of happened."

"Spare me the details, Peyton. Clay is nothing but a joke."

Once again, irritation, followed by anger, flooded me. It wasn't a wonder I never told Knox anything but lies. When this was the reaction, I always got in return, no matter if I told him the truth or not.

"You might think that Knox, but let me tell you, he

is so far above and beyond the guys I've dated. He's a man—"

"I don't want to hear it, Peyton. In my books, Clay Harris is nothing but a fool, and he is dead to me from here on out."

"You know what, big brother…you best watch who you are talking about, but that fool that's dead to you is the father of my baby. Now, I've got to go. Oh, and don't bother to pick me up from the airport on Friday. I'll have Clay do it."

I ended the call, then shoved my phone into my pocket. I didn't have another thing to say to my brother on this subject, and if I had my way, I'd make sure not to see him when I was in Vancouver this weekend.

Chapter 17

Clay

I PULLED up outside the airport early Friday morning and parked the car. Reese and Lorelai had called me to see if I'd be able to pick Peyton up from the airport tonight and take her back to my place for the night, since Knox was still angry and unbearable to be around. I told them it wasn't a problem since she'd already asked.

I looked over to the door to see Peyton pulling a small suitcase behind her with a bag slung across her body. I quickly jumped out of the car and took off over to where she was, quickly taking both bags from her.

"Clay don't be silly. I've got it."

"I know, and now I have it." I winked.

Once I had everything in the trunk of my car, I wrapped my arms around Peyton and placed a kiss on her lips.

"Good to see you. How are you feeling?" I questioned, placing my hand on the flat of her stomach.

She let out a cute giggle and shook her head. "I'm good. Honestly, I'm glad to be back here. I needed a break from packing." She softly smiled as I opened her door and waited while she climbed in and buckled up.

I walked around the car and climbed into the driver's side and took her hand in mine as I pulled away from the curb.

"Well, you can rest the weekend away. Have you talked to your brother again?"

Peyton had called me after her blowout with Knox over the phone. She was upset, angry, hurt, and it took me forever to calm her down. I'd told her to give it a couple of days and then call him to talk it through, but she refused. She told me that unless he called and apologized first, she'd not do it, and as far as I knew, he'd not called her.

"I don't want to talk about him, please. I want to have a good weekend, watch you play hockey, and get some rest before I return to Vermont and go back to packing."

"Fair enough, but you remember he plays on the same team."

"Don't remind me. I was trying to pretend he didn't, and honestly, if he touches you again, I'll have to hurt him."

She was honestly adorable when she was angry, I thought to myself as I looked over at her. I placed my hand on her upper leg and gave her a light squeeze.

"Are you hungry?"

"Starving," she said, placing her hand on top of mine.

"YOU CAN PUT your stuff in here," I said, opening the top dresser drawer I'd emptied.

"Thanks, but really, you didn't have to. I can just keep everything in my suitcase."

I shook my head. "Not a chance."

She smiled and began unpacking, placing her things inside the drawer.

"You can put your toiletries in the bathroom too. I made room on the right side of the double sinks. Is that okay?"

"More than okay. Thank you, but I feel you've sort

of turned your stuff upside down to accommodate me."

I walked over, wrapping my arms around her, and pulled her close. "I'm definitely not turning my life upside down," I whispered, pressing a kiss to her lips. "The drawer was already empty, and the right side of the sink wasn't being used." I chuckled as I kissed her neck.

She let out a giggle and hugged me tighter before turning in my arms and pressing a kiss to my lips.

"Before you continue unpacking, come with me for a minute," I said, taking her hand in mine.

"Where are we going?"

"You'll see."

We walked down the hall, and when I came to the closed door, I stopped. I put my hand on her lower back. "Close your eyes."

"Clay, what are you doing?"

"Just close your eyes. I have something to show you."

She looked at me and rolled her eyes, then closed them while smiling.

"Okay, keep them closed."

I opened the door and gently pushed her forward, and together we stepped into the room.

"Okay, open them," I said, flipping on the light.

She opened her eyes and looked around the room,

her jaw dropping when she saw what was over against the wall.

"Clay…what is…"

"I had someone come in and paint, and I ordered in a few baby things. Not too much, because I wanted you to have a choice as well. I thought we could organize some of this while you were here this weekend."

I watched as she moved over to where I'd placed some things I'd ordered. A crib and a gliding rocking chair, a change table and a small dresser. She ran her hand along the white crib and then sat down in the glider rocker and looked up at me, tears in her eyes.

"Wow, I can't believe you did this."

"Do you like the color of the room? If you don't, we can have it redone. I've kept the painter on standby. I have the chips in the kitchen. I just chose what I thought would work for both a boy and a girl."

Peyton got up from the rocker and walked over to me, wrapped her arms around my neck, and brought her lips to mine.

"It's perfect. It's all perfect," she whispered as she brought her lips to mine again, this time kissing me deeper.

Pulling her into my arms, I kissed her neck as my hands explored her body. As I gripped her ass, gently nibbling on her bottom lip, she let out a moan. I lifted her up, and supporting her ass with my hands, I carried her down the hall toward my bedroom and placed her on the bed.

I knelt beside her, laying her back, undoing one button at a time on her shirt until it was open. I ran my hand down the center of her chest, down to her navel, and flicked the button on her jeans open.

She looked up at me. I could see the want, the hunger in her eyes. I felt her hand run along the inside of my thigh and then over my aching bulge. Heat ran through me as she gently squeezed my cock.

"I want this," she whispered, her eyes innocently watching me.

I flicked the button on my jeans open and unzipped them, giving myself a little room, and bent down and kissed her lips as her hand slipped into my pants.

"I want you," I whispered. "All of you."

She undid the front clasp of her bra, and the moment I saw her hard pink nipples, I bent down and took one in my mouth, sucking and teasing her with my tongue and teeth. I gently bit down, only to have her jump a little as she inhaled.

"Did I hurt you?" I questioned, running my thumb over them.

"They are just a little more sensitive than normal," she said, her cheeks flushing with color.

"Perfect," I whispered, taking one into my mouth again.

She let out a low moan, arching her back off the bed as I gently sucked, then moved to the other side, sucking that one into my mouth.

"Feels so good." She moaned, running her fingers through my hair.

I stood up, dropping my pants, and pulled my shirt off while Peyton did the same. As she scooted into the center of the bed, I turned, and that was when she caught sight of the bruise on my ribs.

Immediately, she reached out and placed her hand over my ribs. "What the hell happened?" she cried.

I'd forgotten about the bruise, about the kick.

"Don't worry about it," I mumbled, crawling into bed and taking her in my arms, kissing her.

I held myself up, resting on my forearm as my hand explored her body. I drew circles on her belly, lowering down and peppering her stomach with light kisses as she ran her hands through my hair.

I ran my hands down her legs, my fingers skimming over the skin of her inner thighs as I watched her. She was beautiful. She lay there with her eyes closed, biting her bottom lip each time I brought my fingers close to her center.

"You want that baby?" I whispered, drawing my fingers up again.

"Please," she cried.

I drew my hand away, slowly bringing it back up,

only to draw it away again as she squirmed under me, a small whimper escaping her lips.

"Please, Clay, don't tease…"

The moment she said the word tease; I gave her what she wanted and ran my fingers through her slick center. The moan that escaped her sent a wave of excitement through my body, causing my cock to throb.

As my fingers danced over her clit, I felt her hand take hold of my cock and stroke it.

"God…it feels so good," I whispered as she took her thumb and smeared the bead of pre-cum that had formed over the head of my cock.

She pushed me back until I was lying down on the bed, then she scooted down and took me into her mouth. I ran my fingers into her hair, resting my hand on the back of her head as I watched her take my cock to the back of her throat repeatedly.

She looked up at me, wiped her mouth, and then straddled me, bending and kissing me as she slid down onto my cock. I gripped her hips and focused on her breasts as she rocked her hips back and forth.

"Remember what I said to you the first night?" I asked, breathlessly as I tried to hold back my release.

She nodded, looking down at me, her eyes filled with want and need.

"What did I tell you?"

"That this pussy belongs to you," she whispered.

"Does it?" I questioned.

I could feel my release coming faster than I wanted it to. I could already feel her tightening around me. She began rocking faster, and I held her hips hoping to slow her pace.

"It does…" she cried. "Only to you."

Chapter 18

Peyton

"WHERE ARE WE GOING?" I questioned as Clay came out of the bedroom dressed in a nice pair of jeans and a sweater.

"I told you. We're headed to dinner, and before you ask, you look perfect," he said, walking past me and slipping his feet into his shoes.

I'd worn the only sweater I'd brought and a pair of jeans. I looked down at myself and pulled a piece of lint off my sweater before slipping my feet into my shoes as well.

"Yes, but where for dinner?" I questioned. "I wish I had brought something a little dressier."

"You'll see." He smiled as he held my coat for me to slip into.

After our afternoon romp, we'd showered and then got ready to go out for dinner. I sat in the passenger's seat as he drove through Vancouver, finally turning into an area I recognized.

"Wait, where are we going?" I asked again, this time knowing full well where he was headed.

"Well, Lorelai called, and she and your mom wanted to have us for dinner."

Anger flooded me. This felt like a bit of a setup. Neither of them had called and spoken to me. Instead, they talked to Clay.

"No way. I told you, I'm not stepping foot in my brother's house until he apologizes, and I don't want you to go in there. He's apt to kill you."

"Look, we are going to be adults about this. We've been invited to have dinner with Dylan, Aurora, Candance, and Phil, and your mom, Lorelai, and Knox. He'll behave. He will have too many witnesses otherwise." Clay chuckled.

"You don't get it. I want him to be the bigger person and to accept things for what they are. I want him to apologize to me. I won't go begging him for an apology. He was absolutely awful to me and look at what he's done to you."

"That is what we all want. So that is what this night

is all about," Clay said, pulling into their driveway.

I sat there staring at the house, anger coursing through me. I didn't move as Clay climbed out of the car, nor when he opened the door. Instead, I waited until he placed his hand inside, waiting for me to take it, but when I didn't, he cleared his throat.

"Peyton, come on," he said. "Let's be an adult. This will pass over."

"You're impossible," I muttered as I reluctantly undid my seatbelt and climbed out of the car. We walked up the walkway to the door, where Clay rang the bell. It was only a couple of moments before the door was opened and Lorelai smiled.

"Come in, you two. Don't worry, the big bad ogre isn't here yet." She winked as we both stepped inside.

Immediately, she wrapped her arms around me, giving me an enormous hug.

"I'm so glad you came," she whispered. "I'm sorry my other half is such an ass."

"No need for you to apologize. I know what my brother can be like."

"Well, things are going to be remedied tonight," she said, taking my coat along with Clay's. "Come on in. Dylan called. Aurora isn't feeling great, so they are staying home, but Candace and Phil are in the kitchen with Reese." She winked.

Clay didn't wait. He placed his hand on my lower

back and guided me to the kitchen where, the moment my mother saw me, she came right over and wrapped her arms around me.

"Darling, how are you feeling?" she questioned.

"Fine, Mom, don't make a fuss, please."

Mom hugged me again and then shook her head, turning to Clay. "Hey, Clay. I'm glad you got her here."

"Of course," he said, hugging Mom quickly and then letting her go.

"Your eye is looking much better," she added. "I can't believe my son actually did this to you."

"If you think that is bad, you should see his right side," I muttered.

Mom looked at me and then back at Clay. "What did he do?" she questioned.

"Don't worry about it. That remedy you gave me worked wonders. I've had so many black eyes and nothing has ever worked as well as what you gave me. I'll try it on my ribs."

"I'm glad it worked well for you," Mom said, smiling. "I'd like to see your ribs though."

"No need, really. It's almost healed."

I shook my head as I watched Clay shake hands with who I imagined was Lorelai's brother Phil before he turned and introduced us.

"Hey, Peyton, nice to finally meet you," Phil added,

coming over and pulling me in for a hug, then he turned to his wife and introduced me.

"Nice to meet you." I smiled.

"We've heard lots about you," Phil added. "And we won't judge you based on anything Knox has told us."

"Thanks." I smiled, leaning into Clay while he placed his hands on my upper arms and rubbed them.

"Have a seat," he whispered. "Want a water?"

I nodded and took a seat.

"How is the packing coming?" Mom questioned.

"Good, just about done. Hopefully, only another two weeks, and then everything will be ready." I smiled.

"Perfect, and I wanted to let you know the apartment will be ready by then as well."

"Great."

We talked a little about things while we laid in bed last night, and Clay had expressed an interest in living together when I moved here. I wasn't sure if now was the time to tell my mother or not. I looked over and met Clay's eyes, but he only subtly shook his head, so I said nothing more.

"So, Aurora isn't feeling so good?" I questioned.

Lorelai looked over at me and shook her head. "No, she was having some slight contractions today at work, so we sent her home early. She still wasn't feeling too great tonight, and her doctor told her just to rest. I told her she should be off now, but she's stubborn."

"I hope she is okay."

"She'll be fine," Mom added. "Dylan will call if anything happens. Lorelai made sure of that."

Lorelai let out a laugh and nodded. "That I did."

"I'm home. Everyone ready to eat?" Knox yelled as he shut the front door.

I looked over at Clay, who came over to where I sat and stood behind me, placing his hand on my shoulders to comfort me. He placed a kiss on the top of my head and whispered in my ear that everything would be fine.

"Yep, bout time you got your ass home!" Phil yelled, winking at me.

"God, who the hell invited you?" Knox chuckled as he came around the corner, a smile on his face, until he laid eyes on Clay and me.

"What the hell are you two doing here?" He frowned. "Lorelai, a word, please."

Lorelai glanced over at us and rolled her eyes and followed Knox down the hall to the bedroom, where we heard the door slam. Muffled voices carried down the hall for a bit, and then Lorelai appeared, her eyes red and glassy.

"Ready to eat?" she said, smiling through what I was sure were tears as she nodded toward the table.

"Clay, Peyton, how about you take the seats down there? Phil, Candace, how about you guys sit across from them? Reese, please take the seat beside Peyton. I'll sit here, and Mr. Grumpy Pants can sit at the head of table." She winked in my direction and gave me a fake smile before heading to the kitchen, where she began bringing full dishes to the table.

The moment she sat down, Knox appeared and took a seat without so much as even glancing in our direction. The table was quiet as the food was passed around, and once all the main dishes were back in the center of the table and we'd dug into the food, Phil cleared his throat. I glanced over at Clay, only to feel his hand on my thigh and give it a gentle squeeze.

"For fuck's sakes..." Knox muttered under his breath. "If I'm going to be forced to allow you to eat at my table against my wishes, the least you could do is respect where you are and not grope my sister. After all, I think you've done enough," Knox muttered.

I could feel tears welling in my eyes at Knox's words. I looked over at Lorelai, who sat there with a frown on her face and a look of disbelief. Phil then met my eyes and cleared his throat.

"How are the wedding plans coming, Lorelai?" Phil questioned, as if nothing had just happened.

"Fine, we are trying to still decide on invitations and cake flavors."

"Oh, have you narrowed it down?" Candace asked.

"I have picked three invitations and two cake flavors. It's my other half who is undecided. He doesn't like any of my choices."

"I never said I didn't like your choices. I said it really didn't matter to me which invitation you chose. However, you know my feelings on the red velvet cake," Knox muttered, keeping his head down.

"I just wanted your input. It's your wedding as well," Lorelai said, glancing across the table at us.

"Jesus, can't anyone just do what I tell them to. I told you I was fine with the invitations, any of them. Pick one. The cake, I wanted vanilla, not butterscotch, not that stupid orange, whatever it was called, and I hate red velvet. As for the meal, put the damn choices down on the card and let the guests decide what they want to eat."

I looked over to see Lorelai was now really on the verge of tears. My mother wore a shocked expression, and then I glanced over at Clay. It was at that moment that Knox threw his napkin down on the table and stood up.

"Where are you going?" Mom questioned.

"I'm done."

"Done what?" Lorelai asked.

"I'm done with this meal. It clearly doesn't matter what I want, or who I want to share meals with. It was as much as told to me twenty minutes ago down the hall what I was going to do. So, I'm done. I'm going out."

Knox took off toward the door, and seconds later, we all jumped when we heard the door slam shut.

"I'm so sorry. This is so embarrassing," Lorelai cried, while Mom did her best to console her.

"I'll go after him," Phil said, getting up from the table.

We heard the door close moments later. I'd lost my appetite. I knew this outburst was because we were here, and I felt terrible for Lorelai, who'd worked so hard on this wonderful meal.

"I think considering everything, Clay and I are going to go," I mumbled.

"No, Peyton, please don't leave," Lorelai said. "Eat your dinner. I invited you here, and therefore you're allowed to be here. I should have cleared it up with him and told him what my plans were, to have the two of you to work things out. I figured dinner would be a good time to do that. I'm so sorry that the pair of you had to witness this."

"Lorelai, don't you worry. I've seen this man throw plenty of fits over the years. One more will not change my thoughts on him now. He's angry, he's hurting, and I'm sure he feels betrayed," Clay added. "He'll also get over it."

"Yeah, but he's doing this to you. Someone who has lost so much already. He should be happy for you that you have found someone who makes you happy."

"I know in my heart he will be once he gets over everything. Somehow, I knew he'd react this way to the news. I'm sure he thinks Peyton is just another notch on my belt, but he is so wrong," Clay added.

"Well, I'm glad to know that," I whispered.

Cadence, Mom, and Lorelai all laughed at what I said, while Clay took hold of my hand in his.

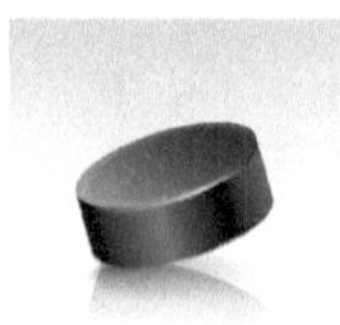

"GUESS I'll see you in a couple of weeks," Clay said, his forehead resting against mine as he squeezed my side, kissing me.

The rest of the weekend had flown past, and while nothing had gotten resolved at dinner that night, I'd wondered what the meaning behind Clay losing so much meant. I finally broke down and asked him on Sunday morning, and he shared his story with me. It broke my heart knowing what he'd been through. Shortly after, he'd promised me he'd work on talking with Knox at the next practice. They had two games left of the second round, and they were down by one game, so if they didn't win the next one to tie it up, they would be out of the playoffs.

"Maybe wait until after you guys play the next game," I whispered, not wanting to bring more stress to the team than was already present.

"Why?" he questioned. "I'm only going to talk with your brother."

"If you talk to him before the game, and then you lose, he will blame us even more for the loss. Please, just wait."

"Alright, I'll wait," he said, pressing his lips to mine. "Don't stress over it. Things will work out."

Chapter 19

Clay - Four Days Later

"THIS BOX IS READY TO GO!" Peyton yelled from one of the upstairs bedrooms.

I climbed the stairs to find her taping one of the last boxes shut. I walked over, grabbed the box from the bed, and carried it downstairs, where I placed it in the hallway. I'd flown out after we lost the last game, sending the Boston Enforcers to the playoffs.

I didn't think it really surprised many of us. We'd been struggling as a team, for the better part of the end of the year. Phil had retired at the beginning of this season. Then Levi and Colton joined the team, mid-season, throwing our entire game play strategies off. I think we'd all been surprised that we'd made it to the second round of playoffs, but when we got the news that Aurora had gone into labor the day before our last game, I think we all knew we were going to lose.

Instead of staying back in Vancouver, I immediately booked a flight to come out here to help Peyton pack up the rest of the things and get ready for the movers. I'd been here two days, we'd accomplished a lot, but we still didn't have any word on how Aurora was.

I went back up the stairs, grabbing two more boxes Peyton had packed, and was about to head down the stairs when I heard a knock at the front door.

"I'll be back for these," I said, heading down the stairs.

I was about to pull the door open when it burst open, and Lorelai walked in. Her hair was pulled back, and she wore the pink jogging suit she loved.

"Hey, more help is here!" she said, smiling, only I noticed it didn't reach her eyes.

"We weren't expecting you," I said, shutting the front door, but when I felt resistance, I stopped.

Knox came in behind her, an irritated look on his face. He walked past Lorelai and headed straight for the kitchen. Then he turned and looked in my direction.

"You weren't expecting us because we weren't going to come, but Lorelai forced me," he mumbled, looking at the boxes that were piled in the hallway.

"Peyton!" Lorelai called from the base of the stairs.

Peyton came around the corner and glanced down at us, a look of shock quickly replaced with a smile as she saw Lorelai.

"What are you doing… here?"

"Well, we thought you could use some help. So, we flew in first thing this morning. "What can I do?" she said, shedding her jacket and placing her hands on her hips.

"Well, if you want to come up and help me here, I am just about done with the last bedroom, and then we can get started in the kitchen. This may go faster than I thought," Peyton said, sounding excited to almost be finished.

"Outstanding," Lorelai said as she climbed the stairs two by two. "Don't you two kill one another. Hear me, Knox?"

Knox muttered something under his breath as he looked in my direction, shaking his head. I chuckled and took off to grab the two boxes I'd left at the top of the stairs and made my way back down and into the kitchen.

"The moving pod should be here any minute. We can get some boxes loaded and out of the way as soon as it arrives, which will make it easier to move around," I said, pulling two beers from the fridge, handing one to Knox. "Let's go out back, shall we?" I said, opening the back door. "I can use a quick break."

"How big of a bin is coming?" Knox questioned, taking a swig of beer, closing the door behind him.

"Well, I ordered it based on how many rooms this place had, so they assured me everything should fit into one."

"When will it be on its way to Vancouver?"

"The day we head back to Vancouver, Saturday morning. It's scheduled to be picked up at eight in the morning. We fly at three. What about you guys?"

"Same. It was the only flight Lorelai could get, apparently."

I could feel the tension between us. The same tension I'd felt that night at dinner, on the ice, even during our last game. It was different, though, from that day in the locker room when he'd hit me. Yet I was still tired of the tension. I knew he was angry, but this had to blow over, and it needed to blow over now.

"Any news on Aurora and Dylan?"

Knox shook his head. "Nope, Lorelai messaged before we got on the plane this morning. Still nothing."

I nodded, taking another swig of my beer. Tension continued to build, and we stood in the backyard like we were strangers instead of friends.

"Look, can we just clear the air? I can't take this anymore, this barely speaking to one another."

Knox sat there, arms resting on his knees, hands wrapped around the bottle he was drinking from, looking down at the ground.

"I don't want this to ruin our friendship. You guys are all I have," I said.

"Look, I've had time to think things through, and I will admit, I flew off the handle a little and didn't keep a rational, levelheaded mind. Peyton hasn't made sound choices lately, you know that. The guys that she's dated have always used her, some doing an awful lot of damage I'm sure, even though she hasn't seen it. I was afraid when I found out that she was pregnant that you too would eventually just walk, that maybe you had been using her."

"I get that, and I can certainly see where you are coming from. Most guys would bail."

"Damn straight they would. I've known you a long time, and I've known your track record…"

"Yeah, and don't forget, I know yours, but I've never gotten a girl pregnant, at least not that I know of, anyway."

"Nor have I," Knox added. "I guess I just jumped to conclusions that you'd do what probably all the guys she's dated would do. It was wrong. I shouldn't have assumed."

"You are right. You shouldn't have assumed shit. I'll admit, I won't lie, I was scared, and after she told me. I contemplated just disappearing, but when it came down to it, I also knew how I felt about your sister. It was something like the Dylan-Aurora situation. So, while I was scared and I wanted to run, a huge part of me knew I couldn't. I'll always do right by her, I promise you that."

"I know Lorelai has beat that into me. She said she was tired of my irrational attitude. She also told me I wasn't being fair to either of you."

I couldn't help but chuckle. "Sounds like Lorelai, but she is right. I'm surprised she hasn't cut you off."

"Buddy, you seriously have not got the faintest idea."

"Uh-oh, what happened?"

"Well, the night of the dinner when I lost my shit, once everyone left and I returned, in the privacy of our bedroom, she gave me my ring back." He said, avoiding my eyes.

"What?" I gasped. "No."

"Yep, she basically told me there was no way she was marrying someone as pig-headed as me. So, I spent the night alone for the first time since she'd moved in, and let me tell you, it's been the worst night's sleep I've ever had. She's been sleeping in the guest bedroom ever since."

"Is that why she's a little off?"

"Yep, I've tried to talk to her to get her to reconsider, but she's as much as told me that once we get this move for Mom and Peyton out of the way, she'll be looking for her own place again. I firmly believe that if Mom hadn't been staying with us, she'd have moved out already."

Knox looked so defeated, I truly felt bad for him, but I also knew Lorelai wouldn't take his shit either.

"So, is that why suddenly you're willing to talk?" I questioned.

Knox shrugged. "That and other things. Phil gave me shit. He told me I needed to remember who Lorelai really was, his sister, and that I really had no room to talk. Then, my mother gave me a piece of her mind too the following morning and then told me I was acting worse than my father ever would have been. That struck a fucking chord with me because, as you know, he was terrible, so when I heard that, I sort of gave things a second thought."

"So, you pulled your head out of your ass?"

"You could say that. I also hated being told I was worse than my father. My entire life, I've worked hard to be better than him. I think that was why I cared so much about Peyton and her decisions. I need to remember that she is an adult."

"She is, and I swear to you once again that I'll always do everything in my control to do right by her."

"I know you will. I never should have doubted it, man. Seriously, I should have known that, out of everyone, after what you've been through losing your entire family, that you'd do right no matter what, especially if you had feelings for her. Ultimately, what happens is between the two of you. It has nothing to do with me."

Knox surprised me by standing up and giving me a quick bro hug, but he quickly pulled away right after because the back door opened.

"Well, no one is bleeding," Lorelai said, stepping into the backyard, followed by Peyton.

"Thank god for that." Peyton smiled.

Peyton glanced over at her brother and, without another moment being spared, Knox walked over and hugged her.

"Just wanted to say I am sorry for how I acted. I'm happy for you, and if you want to be with this loser, then by all means, go for it. But don't say I didn't warn you."

I looked to the ground and smiled as Peyton hugged Knox and then placed a kiss on his cheek.

"I love you, kid, no matter what you might think. I'm sorry for the things I said to you."

"I love you too," Peyton said.

When he let her go, he walked over to where he'd

been standing and picked up his beer, taking another drink.

I turned to Peyton and took hold of her hand. "I've had enough of a break. Let's go get the rest of the boxes from upstairs. I think these two need to talk."

Peyton only nodded and then slipped her hand into mine. I was certain she already had heard everything from Lorelai.

Chapter 20

Peyton - Three Months Later

IT'S BEEN a little over three months since I'd moved to Vancouver. My plan had been to move in with Mom when I'd first moved here. The place she found was an equal distance between Knox and Clay, but once I got here, things changed.

Clay wanted to be involved in all medical appointments, he also didn't want to miss anything, and once he'd patched things up with Knox, there was no holding him back. The first thing he did was ask me to move in with him. I took some time to think about it, talking things over with my mother, and then finally said yes.

I walked up to the door of the Sip and Stir and pulled it open, immediately spotting Lorelai in a booth against the wall with Aurora and Ellie.

"Hey!" I smiled, taking a seat beside Lorelai.

"Morning," Aurora and Ellie said in unison.

"All unpacked?" Lorelai asked.

"Yes, finally. The only thing that would have made it easier would have been if Clay had asked before we had everything dropped at my mother's." I giggled. "I'm seriously happy to be home here, though."

"Well, get used to it. These boys do nothing in the order it should be done. At least you had the help from Knox, Lucas, Dylan, Levi, and Colton, and Clay. You probably didn't have to lift a finger," Aurora added.

"Nope, all I had to do was tell them where to put boxes." I smiled.

"That's good, and Knox was on his good behaviour?" Lorelai questioned.

They had patched things up before returning from helping in Vermont those couple of days. That had been a blessing because poor Lorelai had cried on my shoulder for the entire time the boys had been outside patching things up, worried that this was the end of them. I knew, deep down, that it wasn't, because I knew they were in love with one another. Plus, I'd kill my brother if he'd not fought for them. He was so lucky to have Lorelai.

"He was. They are getting along way better. What about you guys?"

Lorelai smiled. "Well, the wedding planning is back on. We finally came to an agreement on the invitations —went with a completely different one—and even picked the cake flavor."

"I'm glad to hear that," Aurora added.

"Yes, how is the wedding planning coming for you guys?" Lorelai asked, looking over at Aurora.

"Well, the complete lack of sleep we are both getting is not helping. Jackson hardly makes it a couple of hours before he's awake again. It's been hell, honestly, and he's only been with us for a month. I think Dylan secretly wishes we could just put him back, and all I can say is thank goodness Dylan is off now. At least we can take turns getting up with him."

"Is this really what I have to look forward to?" I questioned, looking at Aurora more closely, noticing the dark circles under her eyes.

"Unfortunately, yes. I just hope that for you, your baby at least sleeps a little longer than Jackson does."

"Me too. By the time he or she is born, Clay will be back in the full swing of practice." I sighed.

"Don't worry, I'm sure between the four of us we will help you," Lorelai added.

"Speak for yourself. You could be pregnant by that time as well." Aurora giggled.

"Only if the man watches his attitude," Lorelai said, balling up the sugar packet and throwing it at Aurora.

"So, what are you guys up to tonight?" Ellie asked. "Lucas mentioned something about dinner out?"

"Yeah, Knox said Clay was taking you to the Sunset," Lorelai added.

"Oh, that is my favorite restaurant. I'm hoping that maybe one of you guys will babysit for us one night, and Dylan and I can get out for some adult time," Aurora said, pulling out a bottle from her bag and holding it for Jackson. "I think we could both use it."

"Get us some dates. We'll figure something out," Ella said, turning her attention to me. "Now about The Sunset?"

"Well, he's been secretive about tonight. All I know is that the place is called The Sunset. Other than that, I know nothing," I added.

"You'll love it. They have the best food. Seriously, oh, and make sure you have the chocolate fudge cake, the one that is covered in roasted coconut. You won't regret it," Aurora added.

"Oh, that is my favourite too. I tried it after you told me about it." Lorelai giggled. "Maybe I should talk to Knox about seeing if they can cater the dessert at our wedding instead. That would be such a hit, although he'd probably be irritated that I'm wanting to change my mind."

"Sure would be!" Aurora added. "What about a sweets table for later?"

"Great idea!" Ella exclaimed, taking a sip of her coffee.

Once on the topic of desserts and weddings, we began talking more about Lorelai and Knox's wedding. We also set a date to try on bridesmaid dresses, and by the time I left, we'd also set up our first girls' night. Nothing big, just dinner and drinks, but it was something for the four of us to look forward to.

I SAT across from Clay in the restaurant, the entire room bathed in dim candlelight. It was already dark, and we could see lights from the ships in the harbor. It was the prettiest view I'd ever seen.

I took a sip of my tea and took a bite of the chocolate fudge cake that had been recommended to me this afternoon.

"Well? What do you think?" Clay asked.

I opened my eyes and swallowed, savoring the sweet flavor of the cake.

"So good. Honestly, I'm glad Aurora mentioned this, otherwise I'd have ordered the lemon cake, and I think I'd have been disappointed."

"There is no disappointment when it comes to cake." Clay winked.

I dug my fork into the cake and took another mouthful. "You're so right. There really isn't." I giggled.

"You have chocolate on the corner of your lip," Clay added, pointing to his mouth.

I reached up and wiped at my lip, but Clay only smiled when I was finished.

"Lean forward. You missed."

I leaned forward and Clay took his napkin and wiped away the chocolate.

"How did you enjoy dinner?" he questioned.

"I think it was the best meal I've ever eaten. I've never seen shrimp that size before, and the steak was so tender I could have cut it with my fork."

"Yeah, the shrimp are crazy huge." He winked.

"I just…I don't understand why such an expensive place?" I questioned, not used to being treated like this.

"Well, first, get used to it. I know you're feeling a little uneasy." He winked.

I smiled. It made all the difference that he knew I was feeling uncomfortable.

"I wanted tonight to be special. We haven't officially had a real, intimate evening out because of all the work that needed to be done getting you here. Now that you are here, I wanted to change that. I want to wine and dine my girl," Clay said, placing his hand on mine.

"So, I need to get used to this?"

Clay nodded. "There is something else as well," he said, swallowing hard.

He looked a little off, like he was nervous. He shifted in his chair and checked his right suit jacket pocket, then his left, then the breast pocket, a shocked look coming over his face as he frantically started searching.

"What is it?" I questioned, watching as he began panicking.

"Give me a second," he said, getting up and heading out of the restaurant.

Minutes later, he returned and took a seat across from me and nodded to the server to bring us two more drinks.

"What were you going to say?" I asked, frowning. "Did you forget your wallet?"

He looked at me and chuckled. "Nope, got that right here," he said, patting his back pocket.

"Then where did you go?"

"Had to make a call…"

I frowned. "You had to make a call on a date with me that couldn't wait until we got back home?"

Clay nodded. It was then he looked behind me, a look of relief coming to his face.

"Peyton, the last couple of months have been crazy. There have been so many difficulties, but finally things are coming together." He took hold of my hand.

"If you ask me, the craziness isn't over yet. Are you going to tell me who you had to call?" I asked, getting annoyed.

I heard Clay's name and looked around, catching sight of Lucas coming toward the table.

"Hey, man!" he said as Clay stood up. They shook hands, and then Lucas looked at me.

"Sorry, sweetie, I won't interrupt. Just wanted to say hello," he said, winking at Clay before taking off.

"That was weird," I muttered as I watched Lucas leave the restaurant.

"Tell me about it. The guy is super weird. Anyway, I want you to know that I have spoken to both your mother and your brother, and they have given us their blessing."

"There blessing?" I asked, swallowing hard. "What for?"

Clay took my hand in his and then reached into his jacket pocket, pulling out a diamond ring.

"Before the baby comes, I need to know, Peyton. Will you be my wife?" he asked.

My eyes burned as I looked at him and then looked toward the door Lucas had exited from.

"He came to bring that to you, didn't he?"

A smirk rested on Clay's lips as he looked at me. "The girls warned you we do most things backward. I forgot it…I was nervous." He shrugged.

I couldn't help but laugh as I looked at him sitting there looking adorably cute and sexy, his cheeks red with embarrassment.

"Clay, I'd be happy to be your wife," I whispered, leaning across the table and placing a kiss on his lips.

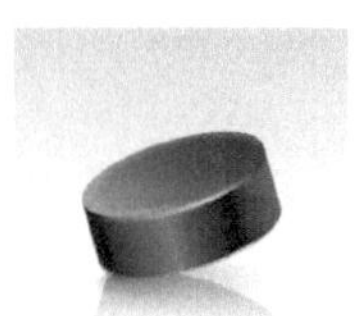

I CLOSED my eyes as he kissed the side of my neck. He pulled the material of my dress and continued trailing kisses down my shoulder, sending tiny waves of excitement through my body.

My center already ached for his touch as his hands came around me and rested on my stomach. I placed my hands on his as he continued placing kisses along the back of my neck and looked at my hand, at the beautiful solitaire diamond ring staring back at me.

In such a short time I'd gone from a broken relationship with my brother because of being in one hell of a shitty relationship with a guy who couldn't care less about me, to finding out I was pregnant. Now I was engaged to a man who I hadn't realized I was completely and utterly in love with. I never realized how fast one could fall in love with someone until now.

I felt the material of my dress fall down my body, the cool air of the room hitting my skin. I pressed my head back against his shoulder. His hand gently rested against my cheek, and he turned my head, meeting my lips. His tongue forced my lips apart, washing through my mouth.

I let out a soft moan as his large hands ran over my bra, gently cupping my breasts.

"I love you." He moaned into my mouth as his hand slid down my body and into my panties.

I closed my eyes as his fingers found my center. "I love you too," I moaned, my voice shaking.

"What do you say we climb into bed, make our engagement official?" Clay whispered, sucking the lobe of my ear into his mouth.

I spun in his arms, wrapped my arms around his neck, and met his lips. I wanted nothing more but for this to last forever, this feeling of us being together.

Epilogue

Clay

The hot sun poured down on us as we sat in Knox and Lorelai's backyard.

"Want to help me get the shade screens up?" Knox asked.

Levi, Colton, Lucas, Dylan, and I jumped up and went straight to work. Within minutes, the backyard was shaded, providing more comfort for not only us, but the girls and little Jackson.

"That is so much better," Peyton said, picking up her lemonade and taking a sip.

"It is. We're lucky it didn't end up raining or we'd

be stuck inside," Lorelai said, bringing out a tray of appetizers.

It was late in the summer for us to have our end-of-season get-together, but at least we'd found a date for all of us to get together. We started up practice in another week, and soon we'd be on the road once again; this year we were determined to win the cup.

"Figures one of the only weekends we were all able to get together it would want to rain. Guess luck was on our side," Ella said, grabbing one of the appetizers from the tray and popping it into her mouth.

"Sure was. Just like this year. We are going to crush it, aren't we, fellas," Colton said, grabbing another beer.

"With all this support, how could we not," Lucas said, wrapping his arms around Ella.

"Support? You mean strict rules," Lorelai added. "That's the only type of support we give, right, ladies."

I couldn't help but chuckle. "I don't know about all you guys, but I'm not living with another coach."

"Nope, definitely not," Knox added at the same time Dylan and Lucas said the same thing.

Colton and Levi both laughed at the four of us. Both were still very single and living the bachelor lifestyle we all once had.

"Keep laughing, you two. We can easily send any one of these girls over your way. I mean, three of them already work for the team, so it's not like they can't torture you as well," I said, pointing at them both.

"They wouldn't dare do that," Colton added.

"Don't bet on it. We love torturing large, grown men, don't we, Aurora?" Lorelai giggled.

Aurora nodded. "I can't wait to get back to work. Listening to men scream is one of my favorite things."

I couldn't help but laugh. I'd been under her torturous hands plenty of times, and I'd always thought she enjoyed every single second of it.

"So, any wedding plans yet?" Aurora asked, looking over at Peyton and me.

"We've decided to wait until after the baby comes," Peyton said, placing her hands on the little baby bump that had appeared in the last couple of weeks.

"Plus, we didn't want to have a third wedding going on in the group at the same time. So, we thought we'd wait until they were over. It will be busy enough what with the guys' schedules, and two weddings this coming year."

"That it will," Knox added. "Not to mention, interviews, promotional opportunities, and all the travel with the upcoming season."

"Exactly. Speaking of interviews, did any of you get contacted by…God what was the name of the magazine?" I asked, pulling my phone from my pocket and opening the email. "Ice Insiders…"

"I did. I sent it over to Pamela to look at it. Any word on that, Ella?" Lucas questioned.

Ella shook her head. "Last I heard, she was still looking into it. She was having a hard time finding information on them. I think they may be new."

Colton cleared his throat. "They aren't new. They may be new to the area, but they aren't new. Ice Insiders was one of the largest publications in hockey when I played for Boston. Their following is quite large, and last I heard, they were trying to expand into the Canadian territory."

"Then why could Pamela not find any information on it?" I questioned.

"Beats the hell out of me. I'm surprised none of you have heard of them. You've heard of them, haven't you, Levi?"

"Oh yeah. I've never been interviewed by them, but I've heard of them."

"Well, they have interviewed me, and I'd suggest, if they reached out, that you take the interview. Who was the reporter? Did it say?"

"A Scarlett Green," Lucas said, looking down at his email.

Levi's head shot up faster than I'd ever seen at the mention of this woman's name. I glanced over at Peyton who had also noticed. She gently took hold of my hand and smiled.

"Do you know her?" Lorelai questioned.

Apparently, Peyton and I hadn't been the only ones who had noticed Levi's knee-jerk reaction.

He shook his head and took a drink of water, then got up from his chair and grabbed a plate of appetizers.

"Nope, never heard of her."

"Anyways, I guess I'll just wait then for Pamela to get back to me, and once I'm given the green light, I'll reach out."

"Sounds good. What do you say we get the steaks on?" Knox questioned.

We all headed over to the barbeque to talk while the girls got busy bringing out the rest of the food. Occasionally, I'd glance over and see Peyton watching me.

Life was good. I was excited about what our future held together, and I couldn't wait to meet our little one. Knox had recently come to me without Peyton knowing, and he thanked me for helping her. We both knew he hadn't been overly happy when we'd gotten together, but he'd seen such a difference in her since he said he had no choice but to put credit where credit was due. Knowing that he truly felt that way had made a difference to me.

Peyton walked over to me, handed me a cold bottle

of water, and wrapped her arms around me, placing a kiss on my neck. "Love you."

"Love you too," I whispered, kissing her lips, then tapping her on the bottom as she took off back into the house to help the girls.

After knowing how much I'd hurt and how lost I'd felt since losing my family, I realized that I belonged somewhere. My teammates were and always had been my family, and I'd added to it with Peyton and our unborn child. I had finally found my place.

Ready for more Vancouver Dominators

Playing the Neutral Zone
Coming June 2025

https://geni.us/PlayingtheNeutralZone

Through the Five Hole
Coming September 2025

https://geni.us/ThroughtheFiveHole

GET A FREE BOOK

Sign up for my newsletter and I'll send you a free book.

https://geni.us/NLSignupBackMatter

Follow S.L. Sterling

Did you know that bookbub has a feature where you can follow me and it will send you an alert when I release a book or put a title on sale? Sign up here and make sure you stay in the loop.

Bookbub:
https://geni.us/SLSterlingBookbub

Website
https://www.authorslsterling.com

Facebook
https://geni.us/SLSterlingFB

Twitter
https://geni.us/SLSterlingTwitter

Instagram
https://geni.us/SLSterlingInstagram

Tiktok
https://geni.us/slsterlingtiktok

Reader Group

About the Author

USA Today Bestselling Author S.L. Sterling was born and raised in southern Ontario. She is married to her best friend and soul mate and lives in Northern Ontario Canada. They have two Alaskan Malamutes.

An avid reader all her life, S.L. Sterling dreamt of becoming an author. She decided to give writing a try after one of her favorite authors launched a course on how to write your novel. This course gave her the push she needed to put pen to paper and her debut novel "It Was Always You" was born.

When S.L. Sterling isn't writing or plotting her next novel she can be found curled up with a cup of coffee, blanket and the newest romance novel from one of her favorite authors.

In her spare time, she enjoys camping, hiking, sunny destinations, spending quality time with family and friends and of course reading.

To be notified of new releases or sales, join S.L.
Sterling's private Mailing List.
https://geni.us/NLSignupBackMatter

Get even more of the inside scoop when you join S.L.
Sterling's private Facebook group, Sterling's Silver
Sapphires: https://geni.us/SapphiresReaderGroup

Books by S.L. Sterling

It Was Always You

On A Silent Night

Bad Company

Back to You this Christmas

Fireside Love

Holiday Wishes

Saviour Boy

The Boy Under the Gazebo

The Greatest Gift

Into the Sunset

Letting You Go

The Spencer Brooks Diaries

Our Little Secret

Our Little Surprise

Our Little Wedding

The Malone Brother Series

A Kiss Beneath the Stars

In Your Arms

His to Hold

Finding Forever with You

Vegas MMA

Dagger

Doctors of Eastport General

Doctor Desire

Doctor Right

Doctor Frost

All I Want for Christmas (Contemporary Romance Holiday Collection)

The Willow Valley Series

Memories of the Past

To Trust My Heart

Letters from the Heart

What Once was Broken

Scars on my Heart

The Happy Holidates Series

Pop Tarts and Mistletoe

Champagne and Fireworks

Summer Nights and Fireflies